Unbelievably Believable

A Miraculous View of This Slice of My Life

Dr. Joyce D. Hightower

Unbelievably Believable

Copyright © *Dr. Joyce D. Hightower, 2025*

All Rights Reserved.

This book is subject to the condition that no part of this book is to be reproduced, transmitted in any form or means; electronic or mechanical, stored in a retrieval system, photocopied, recorded, scanned, or otherwise. Any of these actions require the proper written permission of the author.

Published by Panda Publishing Agency

ISBN: 978-1-80558-372-1 Paperback

ISBN: 978-1-80558-373-8 Hardcover

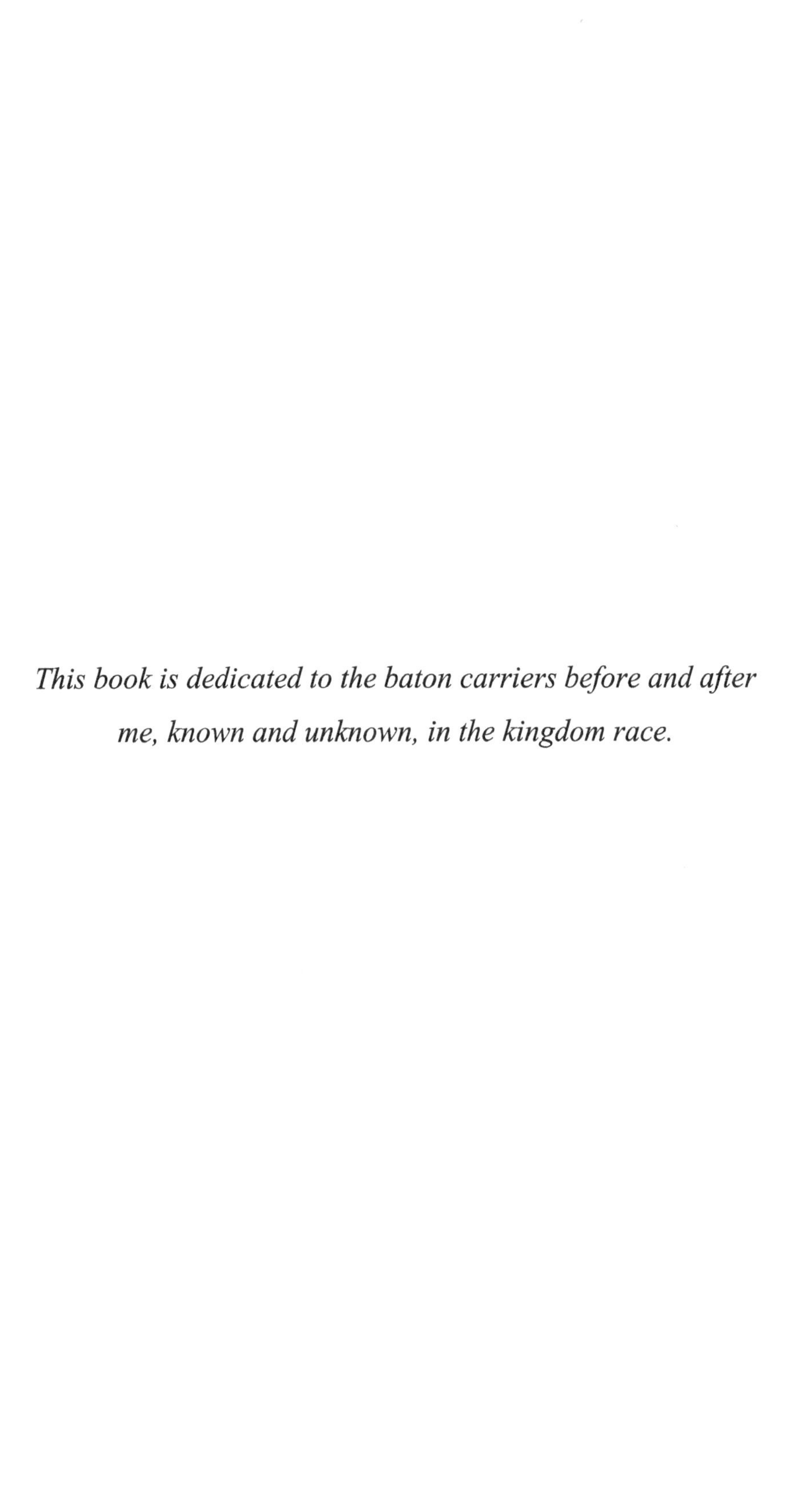

This book is dedicated to the baton carriers before and after me, known and unknown, in the kingdom race.

Foreword

In the Southern California Fourth Ecclesiastical Jurisdiction of the Church of God in Christ, I have served as the Jurisdictional Prelate for over 25 years. The responsibility includes churches throughout Southern California, Belize, Central America, and Ghana, West Africa. I am also on several boards, commissions, and community organizations. As a result of my activities, I know many extraordinary achievers. Joyce is an example for us all. I have watched over her as her uncle, fellow congregant, and believer.

I believe that God blesses us to be a blessing to others. This book focuses on that goal through the eyes of the author and her footprint in our world. Writing the foreword to such an impactful memoir is a distinct honor. It would have been even more inspiring had she chosen to write about more of her life. She has chosen this critical twenty-year period in which she touched the lives of many people in several countries and invested in the future of orphaned children, the health of nations, and strengthening courage in the rest of us.

As a child, I remember Joyce as always curious and adventurous. It should have been no surprise that she would be the first in the family to study overseas during college and then live there as a teacher. When she returned to attend medical school and training despite being a single parent for three young children, she won awards and received applause as she crossed the graduation stage with those three children.

Years later, when we learned of her intent to live and serve in the health system in DRC, we may have asked why she would give up everything again. She was driven, and her focus was a challenge for all who knew her to reconsider whether we had obeyed the call to do what we were meant to do.

In the book, she is open about her thoughts and doubts when facing challenges and decision-making struggles. We observe the calm appearance of a woman full of faith and confidence. But she openly admits mistakes and hesitations. Most importantly, she shares the lessons she learns by allowing us to sit beside her and benefit from her spiritual experiences and discoveries.

She would be invited to speak and share her amazing stories of God's intervention when she came home for a short time. It was always inspiring. After she retired, we traveled together to DR Congo for an annual project inspection. I saw the project compound, met the widows and the people she worked with, and fell in love with the children. The things I saw firsthand gave me a fantastic personal testimony.

Joyce has a long history of providing national and international education and medical services. She also has the talent of a superb storyteller. Listening to her presentations in a church auditorium or over dinner, you feel like you are looking over her shoulder or sitting beside her through the experience. By the story's end, you realize you have been so deeply involved in the message that you are changed when you arrive at the destination. This book is written in the same engaging manner. You will grow to love her friends and understand how she uses negative experiences to gain insight and advance her appreciation of God's love for everyone.

Read this story about Joyce's journey in a world of hard work, wonder, and miracles. You will be inspired to be your best self with God's power. All is possible through the truth God's word teaches us and the power of His love.

Bishop Roy Dixon

Chapter 1

The Democratic Republic of the Congo

"Two years? I thought this trip was planned recently." I shook my head, confused.

"Maybe you planned it recently, but decades ago, our founding prophet said you would arrive this year. Is that why you came? Because of the prophecy?" The journalist's eyes widened.

"Prophecy? No. It was a last-minute decision for me to help with a medical mission. I'm not even supposed to be here," I replied, trying to explain.

She smiled knowingly and nodded. "There are no coincidences with God, Mama Joyce. He arranged everything for you to be here."

A few weeks ago, I'd gotten an unexpected call from a friend requesting I take her place on a medical team to the Democratic Republic of the Congo. Having organized and been part of many such teams in Kenya, my mind was prepared for the usual strenuous schedule. As we flew from Northern California to the heart of Africa, there was no reason to think this would be anything other than a few days of rhythm change from my thankless new position with increasing stressors. But when we landed in April 2001, there was something very unusual in the air, not a smell but a heaviness of expectation with each breath.

On our arrival in Kinshasa, the capital city, the members of our small group of Black Americans were loaded onto the bus and driven into town. Most had yet to travel outside the States, so their eyes were glued to the window, eager to catch their first sight of Africa. With eyes darting to the sides of the road, they pointed excitedly to the crowds of people, dirty streets, open gutters, and over-full taxis still wooing passengers. Women dressed in brightly colored outfits hurried in both directions, stacks of large pots or buckets on their heads with babies cinched on their backs.

Since the bus had no air-conditioning to fight the humid heat, we opened our windows to let in the outside breeze. The smell of rotting fruits mixed with roasting maize and meat accosted our senses. At every traffic slowdown or stop, hawkers rushed into the street between vehicles. Trying to attract buyers, they called out their wares and hurriedly exchanged money for goods as traffic started moving again. Some were barely able to gain safety at the roadside from speeding cars. I had seen this happen in many African countries, from Egypt to Tanzania, but the expressions and comments of my fellow travelers showed they found it nerve-racking. I knew the upcoming clinic activity would soon be so demanding and striking that many of these initial sights would fade from their memories.

We awoke early to depart for our ultimate destination: the city of Nkamba, the headquarters and founding site of The Kimbanguist

Church, our hosts. After breakfast, we embarked on a bone-jarring drive, which took us all day and most of the night. It rained often, leaving the dirt roads muddy and slippery. However, our driver was a master at keeping the four-wheel-drive car on the road and out of the deep ditches along both sides. He was also good at avoiding the most unexpected deep potholes and mounds in the middle of roads created by trucks that had dug themselves out of holes and abandoned the displaced rocks and sand used. We passed small clusters of huts surrounded by lush green farmland. Some roadside produce markets had fruit and roasted maize for sale. The church representatives accompanying us recommended we only eat in sizable towns, where a meal could be purchased from a restaurant. Most of all, there were endless miles of uninhabited land. As the sun set, this greenery was transformed into a monotony of distant horizons meeting cloudy skies and shadowy landscapes often brightened by lightning.

Unable to sleep with the jerking motion of the car, I sang to myself and gazed from my window seat into the darkness. At one point, a bright green light appeared in the distant sky. It descended sharply through the clouds. Then, its direction changed as it rose in an arch-shaped path toward the clouds. Instead of diving to the ground from the top of the arch, this green light completed the other half of the arch's path toward the earth and out of sight. A hill blocked me from seeing its final movement. I was so focused on the object's strange movement that I didn't say anything to my fellow passengers.

As far as the eye could see, the road and surrounding land melded into a sea of darkness and shadows. The only lights were from bright-orange home fires in outside kitchens. Later, not even these were visible. It was only possible to dose intermittently, and we were frequently awakened by the jerking of our vehicle from a dip, bump, or slick, muddy patch.

Finally, the driver's excited voice announced we were nearing Nkamba. Groggy and bump-weary, we sat straight in our seats and peered into the darkness outside our windows, trying to wake up. Our caravan trudged up a hill from a valley of dark huts and dirt roads. We arrived after midnight to find people awake and waiting for us. Crowds lined the road as we drove toward the top of the hill. When we turned the last curve to the summit, a dream-like mansion lit with dazzling electric lights appeared. It sat facing a cement-paved plaza full of a jubilant crowd. Upbeat music blared like an energetic marching band during a football halftime show. It was completely unexpected. I looked everywhere, entranced, trying to see every detail and taking mental pictures. Was I dreaming or entering a magical kingdom at a theme park?

The enthusiastic musicians wearing green-and-white uniforms continued with their rousing music. Hundreds of men, women, and children followed our caravan, cheering as we exited from our cars onto the central plaza area. The flashing camera and crowds made me feel like a movie star. As we followed in a line, crowd members tried to reach out to touch us or shake our hands. Uniformed ushers quickly moved between the crowd and us as we were led to sit in ornate, high-backed, cushioned chairs on two sides of a central aisle. At the head of the aisle were rows of dignitaries facing us and seated in front of the shining mansion. Translators appeared in position at our sides. The assigned guides translated the speeches of the church authorities from the local languages to English, allowing us to keep up with what was happening. After prayers of thanksgiving for our safe arrival, officials gave welcome speeches. During the ceremony, group members were led away individually. I wondered if they had requested a bathroom break when someone whispered something to my interpreter.

My interpreter nodded and whispered, "You are told to enter the residence." I followed instructions and found myself inside the mansion's dining hall. The table was loaded with hot, savory-smelling food, and some other team members were eating and talking.

When I returned to the plaza, the welcome ceremony was winding down. Soon, we were taken to an apartment building down the other side of the hill to sleep. We were informed that a team would ensure that we woke up and ate in time to attend the morning ceremony when we were expected to have something prepared to say. Everyone wanted to hear our voices.

Three of the women among us were designated an elevated status for some reason. We were led up flights of stairs and down a long corridor flanked with doors to what appeared to be apartments. At the end of the corridor, a door opened to a parlor-like room apparently meant for receiving visitors. The next door led to a common area outside our bedroom doors. We were told to keep this door locked at night. After this, we had a lockable separate spacious bedroom with an ensuite bathroom.

***

We were served an early breakfast the following day and then led to front-row seats for the morning ceremony, which lasted a long time. Afterward, I didn't want to return to my room since lunch would be served soon. So, I tried to take in the place's ambiance now that it was full daylight and sans the band or waving crowds. It was quiet as I sat on a short wall bordering the open plaza. I gazed at the Kimbanguist church building looming before me. Known as the Temple, it had been impressive in 1981 when the building, encompassing a thirty-seven-thousand-seat auditorium, was inaugurated. Seeing it standing with its outside walls freshly painted, the church colors white and green, was an incredible symbol of unity. It was hard to imagine that it was built solely by the hands of church members, unaided by machines.

People strolled by, giving shy waves to me or giggling with each other once they noticed me. Around a corner, a tall young woman appeared with confident barefoot steps. Like the other women in the plaza, she wore a wrapped hair covering and a colorful wrap-around skirt. She paused, scanning the place until her eyes settled on me, then approached with a determined stride and soon stood before me and introduced herself.

"Hello, Mama Joyce," she said. "I'm a journalist, and I understand that you speak some French, unlike the others in your group. Can I record a short interview with you for our station?"

I hesitated before answering. *How unusual to be interviewed while on a medical mission*, I thought. My previous typical clinical schedule meant seeing patients from early morning until dusk. That was not the case on this trip. Swallowing hard, I answered, "My French is very rusty, and I must look rough." We had been told on the plane to cover our hair for the arrival out of respect for the church's customs. I didn't understand that this meant my hair should remain covered the entire trip when we were in public. I had one scarf, and it went with my travel outfit. After wearing it for two days on planes, that outfit was in no shape to be worn before a soak-cycle prewash and bleach-augmented wash cycle. I finally decided to use my two-piece light-material suits in the following manner. The blouse would be my headwrap, and the skirt would remain at the bottom. A plain T-shirt would be my blouse. I'd brought extra of these, thinking we would relax in the evening after clinics.

"This is for radio," she assured me. "So don't worry about how you look. People want to hear your voice and your reactions. Don't worry about your French either. I will voiceover what you say with a translation into the local language."

"They will probably call me to eat lunch soon. But we can talk until then," I agreed.

She looked around and pointed to a bus in front of the impressive church building. "Let's sit on the bus. They shouldn't mind." She led the way, mounting the stairs with rapid steps.

I tried to follow her quick steps, but I was too stiff. Having arrived at Nkamba in the early morning, I had only slept a few hours. I felt sleep-deprived and sore from the bus's frequent jerking over the sharp bumps on the rough roads.

"You can sit here." She indicated the seat before her own. Reaching into her bag, she pulled out a small recorder and attached a lapel microphone.

"That's convenient," I commented, pointing to her interview equipment.

"Yes." She smiled, distracted by the setup process. She turned the recorder on and tested it. "Testing. One. Two. Three." She played it back, smiled, and said, "Good. Are you ready to begin?"

"I guess so."

"We are here in Nkamba, the holy city, with Mama Joyce, a medical doctor from California in America." She spoke with a polished professional persona and radio voice. "Mama Joyce, welcome. Can you please state your name?" She turned the microphone toward me and began the usual back-and-forth action as we alternately spoke.

"Thank you. My name is Dr. Joyce Hightower. I'm happy to be here."

"That is great to hear. Can you share more with us? How do you feel being at this holy place full of so much history and many miracles?" She placed the mic in front of my mouth.

"I don't know much about the church. I'm here to learn and help if I can—"

Suddenly, loud crowd roars filled the air as people swarmed the area around the bus. Turning off her recorder, she lowered the window beside her. Leaning out, she yelled questions in the local language to those closest to us, then nodded. Closing the window, she explained. "It's the woman we expected with her dead baby. Papa, the church head, will pray. We'll see if God chooses to bring the baby back to life."

What? I asked myself, caught in a wave of confusion. *Did I misunderstand?* I lowered my window to see for myself. A tearful woman in the center of the crowd was walking toward the church, mounting the hill. She was clinging to a bundle in her arms. The man beside her had his arm around her shoulders like a shield, trying to console and protect her from the crowd. Wave after wave of the crowd surged past the bus from as far as I could see. They marched, waving white handkerchiefs, blowing whistles, or leading cheers.

"Has she come from far away?" I asked, leaning close to hear my interviewer's response.

"She sent word that she was coming three days ago. That's when the baby died."

Chapter 2

It must be my lack of sleep or incorrect hearing. This baby had been dead for three days in the heat of the tropics? Believing that decomposition could be reversed would challenge anyone's faith. And yet she had walked the last three days to get here in an attempt to revive it.

I was going to ask more questions, but she gestured for me to close the window and sit before I could. "Let's continue the interview until news comes about the healing or you are called for lunch." Restarting the recorder, she asked, "How do you feel? What are your thoughts?" Then she aimed the microphone toward me again,

In a long silence, it was difficult to rein in my thoughts and refocus on the interview. Questions, medical impossibilities, and emotional reactions swirled in my head. The journalist reached to switch the recorder off, steadying my swirling thoughts. I gestured for her to wait. "I feel confused by what I see. I'm unsure how things work and why and when you do certain things. Like, you're all barefoot. I don't want to disrespect any rules."

"Yes, we believe the church area is holy grounds. I suggest you follow what your interpreter is doing or ask them for an explanation. We have been training in spoken English for the last two years to be ready to translate for the American visitors expected to come."

"There's a lot to learn and understand," I said, searching the floor for a focus.

She continued to ask questions. Was I married? Did I have children? Then, she asked about my background and family history. She finally seemed to be nearing the end. "Mama Joyce, what would you like to say to the people assembled here for the celebration? Some have come from faraway countries—"

What she said next was drowned out by another wave of people moving in the opposite direction. The returning crowd swarmed toward us. Some near the bus were so excited that they pounded its sides like drums. I stood again, searching the center of the mass. My mind was thrown into a high-speed mental gymnastics effort to explain what I saw. There was the woman I had seen weeping and carrying what I was told was the bundled body of her baby—a baby who had been dead for three days. This woman was smiling, and a living baby was moving and crying in her arms. The same bundled blanket was open and loosely wrapped. Walking beside them was the same father, no longer comforting his wife but rejoicing. My eyes were glued to them, following the group's progression down the hill until they were out of sight.

How could this be true? Was a baby who was dead for three days now a baby alive? My brain could not come up with any explanation for this. But I needed to find one. Even if the baby had been in a coma, appearing to be dead, he could not have gone three days without eating or at least imbibing liquids in this heat.

The journalist yelled so I could hear her above the crowd. "Oh, praise be our God. He has chosen to answer her request. We are blessed to see His grace."

Had I seen a resurrection? In plain view of thousands of witnesses, was this a miracle? Wondering about hundreds of things, I stared at the journalist. *Is that all she is going to say? 'We were blessed to see it'? Did people see miracles so often around here that they were no longer surprised? Were they just thankful to add another miracle sighting to their list?*

"Mama Joyce," the journalist interrupted the Niagara-Falls-like torrent of questions thundering in my head. "I want to get comments from someone who was inside with them. I'll find you again later to complete this interview. Maybe we can do another interview and focus on your plans." She grabbed up her equipment and shoved it into her bag. "I think I saw someone I know over there." She peered out the window to confirm. Then, with her bag strapped over her shoulder, she darted out of the bus.

My jumbled thoughts paralyzed my mind. Deep beneath the surface of my beliefs about the miraculous, a shift of tectonic plates was occurring. The resulting tsunami was heading straight for the nearby shores of my miracle-belief world. My only clear thought was to run. An urge was swelling within me to run as far away as fast and as soon as possible to survive the sweeping changes coming. I desperately desired to leave for higher, safer mental ground, somewhere closer to home, as quickly as possible. Everyone else in my delegation had come with people they knew and trusted to give them feedback. Where was my pastor, close friend, sisters, or mother when I needed them?

"God help me. This is too much," my whisper escaped into the bus's cool air. Warmth was eddying in through the half-opened window beside me, but I shivered. It couldn't be denied or disregarded. Yet, my world had no portal to accept the unexpected, unexplainable events unfolding. Could all the rules of reality change at the same time? Maybe this was a dream. Everything would be clear on awakening. It had worked for Dorothy in *The Wizard of Oz*, right? I sighed, realizing it was more difficult to believe a dream than to think I had entered a place with its own rules. I would have to analyze everything observed and heard.

After all, I was a scientist as well as a Christian, believing simultaneously in creation, a virgin birth, and chromosomes. Closing my eyes, my head rested against my hands, holding onto the solid reality of the seat before me.

Chapter 3

"Mama Joyce," my interpreter's voice called through the window. Standing beside the bus, she looked up, studying me with a crease across her forehead. "Come, Mama Joyce. It's time for lunch."

I followed her into the residence to dine with the rest of the delegation. Over lunch, I asked what they thought had happened to the baby. No one had heard, so I told them what I had seen. They had lots of questions. We discussed what could have happened. No one wanted to be a victim of a sham put on for our viewing pleasure.

Someone pointed out, "If that were the goal, would it make sense for it to happen when you were the only one around."

Another added, "You were out of sight on the bus. They could not predict you'd be there."

The discussion continued about the mom's claim to have left her village three days ago. Anything could have happened along the way. There were fellow travelers and witnesses in the yard on the other side of the church. Could any of them prove it was the same baby? Where were they now? Could we see the baby and talk to the mother? What were some other miracles claimed to have happened in this place? What was the proof?

I didn't have answers. It had been such a shock. I hadn't thought of getting close enough to the baby to see. Discussion continued until silence hovered over us as the table was cleared.

Our intermittent yawning and drooping eyelids showed our weariness as we digested our food and thoughts. From the doorway, an interpreter announced that we were welcome to join the prayer service held every three hours if we liked. However, we compulsorily had to attend an important service in the evening. We were advised to arrive early.

This posed a risk of being late because I did not wear a watch and had no functioning cell phone. I did not know the time, so I asked my suitemates to wake me up. We agreed to leave the suite together to ensure we were all on time. With this assurance, I fell into a deep sleep.

I awoke to see through the window-like space with a small wooden door on hinges that dusk was falling. Having lived on the equator, I knew it was approaching 6:00 p.m. We were to be in our places at 7:00 p.m. I jumped up to wake the others. Knocking on their doors, I got no answers, so I tried again to ensure they were not asleep.

The first door still did not yield an answer despite louder and harder knocking. I tried to turn the door handle, but it was locked. My attempt at the second door also resulted in no reply. However, this door handle turned. I entered the room, hoping to find the inhabitant asleep. Her bed was rumpled but empty. Dim sunlight shone through the open window space. I rushed to knock at the bathroom. There was no answer, so I checked inside, but it was also empty.

The thought that they had broken their promises and abandoned me was upsetting. However, confronting them could wait. I needed to get to the plaza fast. Hurrying back to my room, I closed its wooden window door against the mosquitoes, which were waiting to enter once the sunlight left. I grabbed my purse and rushed through our suite to the hall door. I opened the door and gasped. A chill swept over me as I stared down a long, dark corridor without windows or electric lights.

There was no time for hesitation in choosing between my two options. I could push forward to meet my responsibility despite the danger and fear. I could also justifiably cower in my room because someone had not kept their promise. Closing the door behind me, I felt my way with my hands along the wall into the darkness straight toward the stairwell at the other end. Advancing, I called out to see if anyone was behind one of the doors. I hoped someone with a flashlight would agree to escort me downstairs. In complete silence and darkness, I reached the stairs. Another worry pressed my heart's accelerator.

When we climbed to our room the last two times, I noticed that the granite stairs were uneven in height. One false step could have me tumbling down to an inevitable and significant injury. As I stood on the top stair now, I prayed, "Oh God, please help me not to break my neck."

I slid the heel of my shoe down the front of the first stair. I had seen my blind friend do this many times before. The second step was greater in-depth, and I caught myself falling as I stumbled into the side wall. "Oh God," I prayed. "I need a guardian angel or something. Please help me." I slowly took the next step, bracing against the outer wall this time.

Two flights down, bright lights appeared, emitting enough brilliance for me to see the stairs I was standing on. "Oh, thank God," I called.

The delegation guide called, "Who is that on these dangerous stairs in the dark?"

"It's me, Joyce," I responded. "My suitemates left, and I don't have a flashlight. I'm so happy to see you. What are all of those lights?" I asked, looking over the inner cement wall turn.

"Come join us, Mama Joyce. My new brother and I will wait for you, then we'll tell you about the lights," he said, a large garbage bag of brightly shining lights in each hand.

I hurried to join them. As we descended the rest of the stairway, we shared our activities since leaving the group after lunchtime. After resting, they assembled the solar lights the guide had brought to be placed in the garden. It didn't matter that I had no idea where this garden was located or needed lights. I was so happy that the lights had appeared when I'd prayed. It was my miracle. I'd prayed for light, and it had come immediately. What a fantastic place to live in.

As we talked, we neared the long cement stairway ascending to the top of the church hill. Once we started mounting the steps, we spoke very little. We stopped twice to catch our breath. Just as we arrived at the top, a car parked in front of us. Two of the church officials stepped out.

"I was wondering what to do next," the delegation guide said, "then you pulled up."

They said in unison, "There are no coincidences with God."

Intending to head toward the plaza to question my deserting suitemates, I waved to the delegation guide. But he neared me and whispered, "Please wait a second, Mama Joyce."

"Okay," I agreed and watched to see why he wanted me to wait.

He advanced a few yards to huddle with the two officials and then returned smiling. "They have said it's okay. You can enter to help place the lights in the garden. Come this way."

I did not understand what was happening. But the guide seemed happy and excited. I knew he had been sent earlier in answer to my prayer. The suitemate issue could wait. This was something important. So, I smiled and joined the two brothers again. This time, we followed the two officials to a padlocked gate. The stouter one took a key from his pocket, opened the lock, swung the gate open for us to enter, and then relocked the gate. I was given a bag of lights and told to hand them one at a time to the taller official. The others went to the three remaining corners of the garden. The placement was going smoothly until I realized we were in the area around the mausoleum for the founder. It was intimidating to think of being so close to the burial place of a man whom God had used mightily to start this church in the DRC. The first African-based church to be accepted into the World Council of Churches. There were seventeen million members.

My breath caught when my legs vibrated and quivered as I stepped on the cement square in front of the front door of the mausoleum building. I thought it must have had an electric current running under it. The official I followed did not appear to feel the same effect when stepping on the area. As he repeatedly transversed the square, I scrambled to find a parallel path to hand him the next light. Once, he stopped, stared at me with a big question mark on his face, and asked if everything was okay. I guessed he had noticed all my evasive movements. I nodded yes, and we continued until all the lights were placed. Finally, I thought we were done.

Chapter 4

The white lights against the green bushes made for a beautiful scene. No wonder I had not seen the building before. It had been shrouded in darkness and enclosed with hedges and a fence, but now it was highlighted.

I went to stand by my two delegation brothers. I saw the two church officials praying while standing on that vibrating cement square when I looked around. The delegation guide whispered to me, "Mama Joyce, we believe that the area where you see those two standing is a very sacred spot. You can ask God to grant your desire. It will be granted to you if you ask with a pure heart."

"Oh, I see. So, we are waiting for them to finish. Thank you," I whispered in reply.

"You can go there and pray as well."

"I'm fine," I deferred, imagining myself falling after my legs gave out, leaving me unable to get up. I shivered at the thought.

"Mama Joyce, you do not have to wait. You can go there now." He was determined to have me take advantage of what he saw as a tremendous opportunity.

I could not easily explain my way out of this situation with my quivering legs. I sighed and relented. Then I walked to the cement square and knelt beside the official still praying with his head bowed.

I closed my eyes, and a dome of silence surrounded me. I entered a bright place where, although I saw nothing, I knew God was present and sensed Him listening. I was moved by a deep desire to make it clear my focus was on Him and Heaven. I was that nine-year-old girl in Sunday school again. Overwhelmed by God's love and mercy, I asked Jesus to be my savior. Full of gratitude, I prayed, "God, remember me, Your little servant girl. Supply me with what I need to accomplish Your call on my life. I don't need anything more. Please guide my steps. Lastly, I pray I stand up from this spot without falling." When I opened my eyes, the official was no longer standing there. He had gone without a sound. The din of people outside of the garden was no longer muffled. I was back in Nkamba. The noises of excited people gathering and musicians tuning their instruments in the plaza seemed amplified.

Scrambling to my feet without a problem, I whispered, "Thank God."

I looked back where I had left my two delegation brothers. The two officials had joined them. All four were watching me and waiting. I didn't think my small prayer took a long time, but maybe it did. I have no idea how time works in heaven. Emerging from my extraordinary experience, I hurried over to join them.

"Are you ready to go?" the official with the key asked when I stood beside them.

"Yes, thank you. Sorry for any delay," I apologized.

He unlocked the front gate, and we exited near the plaza area. I walked around the side of the crowd to the chairs in front, which were placed for the delegation.

I caught sight of both my suitemates seated along the rows arranged for us there. Determined to find out why they had abandoned me, I asked each suitemate why they had not awakened me. I was confused when each angrily accused me of planning with the third suitemate to leave her behind. How could all three of us think we had been left behind by the other two? Each had arrived alone.

I knew I had gone into one bedroom and found it empty. When I told one of my suitemates I had entered her room to confirm she was not there, she said something strange. She said she had entered my room to do the same thing and found me gone. She had checked her watch in the light of my open window and saw it was getting late. She hurried back to her room, grabbed her flashlight, closed her window, and headed out. But this was all backward. I had closed my window when I'd left. If she'd found it open, I had to be there still. On top of that was my memory that the window had been open when I'd closed the door to her empty room. Wasn't this an impossible time puzzle?

I asked her more questions, trying to figure out how to get out of this maze. She glared at me and said she did not wish to discuss the situation further.

The person in the room with the locked door said she did not know what we'd thought we were doing by pulling such a mean trick. We had both been gone when she'd left. She said she had checked both our rooms. She did not want to discuss it because she felt she could not trust us. My head was spinning. There had to be a solution to explain all this. Maybe it was one of those time-space dimension mathematical conundrums.

I went down the row to an open seat beside the delegation guide. After telling the story, I asked him, "Can you explain how this could happen?"

He replied, "Listen. Mama Joyce, let me give you some advice. Don't search for explanations of how things happen. God arranges circumstances when he wants something to happen. It can't be explained by logic. He wanted you in the garden and made it happen."

"Do you know why? What's with that garden, anyway?"

"That is the garden surrounding the mausoleum of the founder of this church. One of my assignments for this journey was to bring lights to be placed there. Tonight was a special and sacred time for me to complete the task with the two church officials. Interestingly, God intended for you to be there as well."

"Do you have any idea why?"

"No, Mama Joyce. We'll have to wait until He makes it clear. I asked my brother to help me, and we spent the afternoon preparing the lights. Even then, I thought we would be late, but we were just in time to find you in the stairwell, praying for light. We met the officials before entering, and they agreed to let you in the sacred garden. People are only allowed to enter on special days, but they permitted you to help and to pray at the sacred place."

"Wow. I didn't know all of that," I said and then recounted, "On the stairs, I asked God to keep me from falling and breaking my neck. Your lights came just in time to save me. And we arrived at the same time as the officials right where they parked."

"That's what I'm trying to say. Don't worry about how God does things. Just be glad He has the power. There is something about you, Mama Joyce. He is choosing to work through you."

"I'm trying to grab onto something to stop my feeling of free fall. This place is different from anything I have ever experienced. I've been praying more than ever since we arrived."

"Amen. He will show you." The music started, making hearing ourselves difficult. He yelled, "We'll talk later."

***

Over the next few days, through many conversations, I understood how our delegation's visit was perceived. Decades ago, the church's founder had prophesied that at the turn of the century, African Americans would come to Nkamba. They were to prepare housing in an area called Kindolo. Interpreters were trained to facilitate the entrance of non-French and non-local-language-speaking people into society. As if on cue, we'd arrived by divine appointment. Human beings may have planned our arrival for the maximum political impact, but for all the pieces to fall in place had been above and beyond their control.

During the day, a safety zone was created in the primary residence of the head of the church to protect our delegation's members from the curious masses. This was for our comfort, dining convenience, and daily security. Crowds of people were outside the building on all sides. Many were eager to see us close up. Others wanted to be able to say they had spoken with us. Some wanted to ask for a personal memento of this historic visit or to take a photo with us. People were eager to see firsthand the evidence of prophecy fulfillment and the signal that an earth-changing period was beginning. Our hosts had to, at all costs, prevent any adverse events. In this safety zone, we remained for most of the day. Our delegation was allowed to roam the rooms on one side of the residence's first floor. The other half appeared to be private quarters.

While inside the residence, we discussed the church's history with the church leaders and had questions answered in the lounging room. Most of our delegation assembled there after meals, where a large window gave a clear view of the central plaza. We were allowed to rest between public appearances for ceremonies, church services, and concerts. We also had access to the dining hall, bathroom facilities, and a sizeable reception room called the Hall of Honor.

When we left this building, we were escorted to a specific location as a group. Ushers took us to front-row seats for church services and meetings. Once the last activity of the day ended, we were escorted to the apartment building to spend the night.

Having taken French classes from the seventh to twelfth grade, I spoke French better than my translator spoke English. I asked her to translate the local language, Lingala, into French for me instead of English in the future. This method gave me a deeper understanding of what was being said. Over meals, I overheard others saying inaccurate things they had learned from their interpreters. I tried to explain what they had misunderstood or missed. The responses were mixed.

"You are not the only one who knows a little French, Joyce. If we need explanations, we can ask our interpreters. That is their job. We shouldn't make them feel belittled," one said.

The others' frowns and cast-down eyes showed that this comment had irritated them.

"I think it's good to have the best understanding. I would hate to operate under the wrong information," another group member said. "Thank you, Joyce. I want to hear everything."

It had never been my intention to give the impression of being superior. All I had intended was to help improve understanding, but instead, it had become a point of contention. As a lump rose in my throat, I remained quiet rather than risk crying in front of everyone. After a few minutes, I excused myself and walked toward the bathroom. A tear was already working down my cheek, and I passed the bathroom, searching for a small corner to sit alone for the first time.

To my delight, I discovered a quiet veranda on the backside of the building. The residence had been built on a hillside slope. Although you entered the front at what appeared to be ground level, by the time you walked to the building's rear, you could see it sat above a lower floor. The veranda faced the down-sloping hillside. Surrounded by a molded cement banister, it sat in the shade and out of sight of people walking by. This breezy, quiet spot provided space for undistracted contemplation and was most welcomed by my boggled mind.

After that day, I regularly retreated to this place after meals. However, my desire for solitude brought an unexpected opportunity. People assisting the church officials and leaders discovered my retreat. They came to question me directly, one or two together. I had lots of questions as well. They were not journalists, just regular people curious and eager to share.

They reported knowing nothing of the intended medical mission activity. They explained that people came for prayer healing when their medicine at home had failed. That made sense to me. During the day, Papa or another official often prayed for those in distress who couldn't stand or control their body movements. Some appeared to be having seizures and were carried in. They would undergo a miraculous transformation, their abnormal behavior immediately changing to normal with prayer. Showing no signs of any post-seizure altered state of consciousness, they would stand and walk away clear-eyed with their family members or friends.

So, why had God brought me, a medical doctor, to this place in the DRC? Here, healing miracles happened daily. There was a clinic of some kind. But I had no clue as to what was done there. I had never visited the facility, spoken to the staff, or discussed its plans.

A gnawing feeling persisted at the back of my mind. Something life-changing was imminent, but I had no idea what it was or why. Those around me weren't clarifying anything. I was only getting more confusing information.

On the one hand, I had received no specific instructions regarding my next course of action. On the other hand, there was a constant bombardment of comments about the points of the church founder's prophecies. My demographics matched several descriptions of the American prophesied to usher in the new church period. Resisting the repeated temptation to hear more connecting details was a struggle. These were appealing distractions of pride, intended or not.

This battle of pride has been evident in the lives of the rich and successful throughout history. It has also been seen in people experiencing poverty and failure who are deceived by pride. My family and friends included drug addicts and alcoholics. The glittering image of what they had tried to be eluded them. A resulting short-term violent act or long-term continuous action brings death and pain to all involved. It's fatal for a person to try and contort themselves into the shape of others' expectations.

I intend to avoid starting down the path of becoming imprisoned by expectations. I remembered tensing when anxious whispers were heard about my gentle uncle turning up missing again. Then, relaxing when hopeful adults' relieved whispers signaled that he had been found in a hospital. Years had passed without a word from him, and we had accepted that he was gone. He had lived with a projected image he could not achieve and became addicted to alcohol.

The memory of Jesus's death has brought me freedom innumerable times. Why would I exchange the guidance of the Holy Spirit for fickle human fame? If this prophecy were about me or someone I would work with, it would become apparent as time passed. It would not depend on my learning all the points enumerated in the prophecy and trying to fit into them.

Chapter 5

The head of the church, affectionately called Papa, was the last living son of Simon Kimbangu, the church founder. He received us in a private audience in the Hall of Honor. Located at the heart of the building, it was spacious and brightly lit with an air of international elegance. It was decorated in grand style, from the curtains to the chairs, with white, gold, and deep green colors. Stately oversized armchairs were arranged in a semi-circle facing a single grander armchair where this small, frail man sat in the seat of honor. He had a tremendous scar extending across his scalp from side to side. He spoke hesitantly, and his right hand rested near his knee in constant motion, known as the pill-rolling tremor. As a physician, I had seen these symptoms as signs of Parkinson's disease. I wondered if it was the result of the injury to his head. My medical brain was asking many questions on this day.

Meanwhile, our delegation leader, kneeling in front of him with utmost respect, spoke in hushed tones as she introduced our members to Papa individually. We saw everyone approaching him kneel out of respect. In other African countries, I had seen the same sign of respect shown to people of advanced age or position. Although some in the group were physically challenged by age or stiffness, we knelt before Papa, as tradition required. It was also out of a desire to show an understanding and appreciation that we were being housed, fed, and welcomed at his direction.

His translators knelt beside him, alternating the job of translation. When I was introduced, he asked for confirmation that I was a medical doctor. My reply was yes.

The delegation leader told the interpreters to clarify that I had come as her assistant to avoid confusion. The furtive whispers among Papa's interpreters were not translated to us. After our introduction and greeting, we returned to our seats. Papa welcomed and blessed us. Some discussion among the interpreters was quashed with one word from Papa, and we were dismissed from the formal setting.

We later learned that Papa had declared the prophecy had been fulfilled. He had reminded them he had been promised to live to see the prophesied African American return. This person would herald the return of African Americans to make Africa what it was supposed to be. They would work with those who had remained. How intriguing to think we were in an actual prophecy fulfillment. It had to be someone in our group. This made me look at each person a little differently.

***

The second time I had an audience with Papa was when our delegation head summoned me for a presentation to the church. As expected, she kneeled at Papa's feet, and the ushers told me to join her. Two containers the size of boxes used to transport apples were sitting on the ground beside her. Once I was on my knees, she presented them, saying they were full of medications for use in the clinic. The boxes were sealed shut, so I never knew what was inside.

Papa expressed his gratitude and said that the head of the clinic would come and collect them.

I was disappointed to hear two things. The first thing was the existence of a nearby clinic that we had not visited. The second thing was the lack of any mention of medication needs. It was a shame that neither more medication nor medical services had been offered for this mission. I would have been happy to bring a second suitcase full of medicine. Papa shook the delegation leader's hand as usual at the end of an interaction. She rose and followed the two people carrying the boxes out of the room.

I reached to shake Papa's hand, expecting him to shake my hand and release me to depart. Instead, he continued his grasp. He asked when they could expect me to come and live there.

In hindsight, I should have tempered my response, but the medication donation raised my anger. "I'm not coming to live in the DRC. There were too many responsibilities back home."

He asked what those responsibilities were. I listed the first five that came to mind, including support for my youngest child's university studies. Papa nodded his head and closed his eyes for a minute. I thought he had dozed off, but then he smiled. Opening his eyes, he told me to tell a specific church official about this list, then shook my hand in a release.

Realizing no clinics would be conducted, my disappointment was profound. I tried to recover, but it only increased after questioning the other delegates. No one in the delegation had heard anything about planned medical care activities. *I had wasted ticket money and vacation time. There was never a plan for clinics.* I felt like window-dressing for an agenda I was unaware of.

The church official to whom Papa had told me to give my list of responsibilities passed by me in the hallway. I stopped him and told him what Papa had said. He listened, nodded, and walked away. I don't know what I expected, but my stomach knotted.

From then on, I aimed to learn everything about the DRC and the Kimbanguist Church. I asked questions of anyone available, including cleaners and kitchen help. I also began to understand that the church leaders were receiving reports of my every move. At odd moments, officials asked me about things I had discussed with only one or two people. Perhaps I was seen as too curious, and the leaders wanted to know why and in what I was interested.

***

My interpreter asked if I would attend the symphony orchestra and choir practice. Other delegation members were there to be part of the performance. Another member had arrived late because of a demanding schedule. He was a world-famous African American orchestra director who had arrived to direct the world's only all-Black African symphony orchestra. With this information came my discovery that most of the other members of my delegation were members of the same large African American church choir. They had made the trip to participate in the concert to be held with the symphony orchestra. This was an enormous combination of firsts in the music world and would be filmed for a documentary about the trip. A reporter was in the delegation for this reason.

With this information, the fog cleared away. I had misunderstood my role from the first phone call inviting my participation. The trip organizers had never meant for this to be a medical mission. It was to be a musical political activity. The result was to be a once-in-a-lifetime concert. The plans and goals were outside my desires or intentions. I was flotsam on beach waves, carried by the ebb and flow of deeper currents, no more than another body in the window-dressing display. So, I relaxed and enjoyed listening to the music during the choir and symphony orchestra practices. When they were quiet, melodies could be heard outside everywhere.

For me, one of the most spiritually moving experiences in Nkamba was the prominence of music in the church's daily activities. Each of the scheduled prayers during the morning and afternoon began with a song. Acapella groups practiced in many corners, preparing for church service performances. Guitar, flute, and brass groups were scattered around, doing the same. A tour around the compound in the evening was accompanied by lovely musical harmony at each step. It was like strolling through heaven, hearing angelic choirs trying to surpass each other with uplifting melodies. I did not know the foreign words, but the spirit of worship touched my heart. Tears ran down my face as I passed by one group after another, worshipping in music.

When the concert day arrived, the other nonperforming delegation members and I were escorted to the front-row seats. It was a magnificent performance. The vast church building was packed to capacity. The result was beautiful in every way—visually, audibly, and spiritually. I was refreshed after the immersion in the living water of God's musical worship.

However, music was only one of the many unique attributes of the Kimbanguist Church. I was inspired by the church's history whenever I received an answer to my question. Although I had never previously heard its name, it was one of the world's most prominent African indigenously founded Christian churches. Interestingly, the church highlighted the shoulder-to-shoulder role played by women in its running. The church leadership comprised several women pastors and participants. The wife of the founder had called to order the very first service conducted by the church. Since then, no service has started without a woman opening up with a prayer. This was surprising in light of the social rules in Africa, usually relegating women to chattel positions.

***

When I was summoned to meet Papa for the third time, he repeated the question, "When are you coming to live here?"

"I'm not coming to live here. As I told you before, I have too many responsibilities at home," I replied once again. As I spoke, an idea flashed across my brain. "But it might be possible to do a project. As the head of the church, can you tell me what project would be the most helpful?"

When the interpreters relayed my response, Papa smiled and sighed deeply. Instantly, something shifted deeply again in the ground of my faith. Despite his disease and frail condition, he bore this heavy responsibility as the head of this worldwide church with dignity and wisdom. Powerful waves of deep appreciation washed over me as my heart swelled with admiration, and tears filled my eyes. At this moment, I realized Papa had not released my hand. When I looked at his face to see why, his eyes locked my gaze, and I could not look away.

His hand no longer trembled. My body was being slowly lifted off my knees by his single hand. He lifted my heavy body to a curtsy position where I stood on my feet with bent knees, seemingly with little effort. Unable to resist and yet not wanting to show disrespect, I asked those on either side of Papa, with my gaze locked on him, frantically, "What should I do? He's lifting me to stand. I know we aren't supposed to stand in front of him. What shall I do?"

They excitedly replied, "If he is lifting you, you cannot refuse."

The strength of this tiny man was incredible. He could not walk without support. Yet, with one unfaltering hand, he lifted me to a full standing position. Like launching a ship, he gently moved me backward and released my hand. He smiled and broke eye contact. His hand began to tremble, resting on his knee. The following person quickly knelt before him with their request.

Chapter 6

I stood as if glued to that spot, my feet too heavy to move. I waited, wondering what was supposed to come next. Everyone else acted like I wasn't there, stuck, and like everything was normal. *Am I being dismissed or sent away? Am I supposed to leave Nkamba?* I wondered. My legs regained their strength, and I rushed out into the hallway in tears. An interpreter hurried to me, saying a message would be delivered later to explain what I would do next.

I ran to the veranda, my refuge. My stomach felt both full and empty. My eyes were watery, but no further tears flowed. What had all of that meant? It was a mix of sensations, like being handed a debate competition trophy and a graduation diploma. I was happy to have achieved a reward but was sad to leave for the next life level, knowing I could return for visits but would never play that role again.

I waited numbly for a long time, and dusk wrapped a comfort blanket around me. I heard the sounds of the others enjoying the evening meal in the dining room but didn't want to move or talk to anyone. What I wanted, what I needed, was clarity.

Two of Papa's interpreters entered the hidden comfort of undisturbed quiet and cloaked from the sun's last efforts of the day. They looked solemn. This made me more anxious to hear the news. My eyes shifted between their faces. "Tell me what Papa said. Do I have to leave? Why did he push me away?"

"No, No, Mama Joyce," they chuckled, looking at each other.

"Papa said he did not answer your question at that time. He didn't want words to limit what the Holy Spirit would do through you. When you return, you will be guided as to what you will do," the taller one said.

"Oh, thank God," I sighed. "At least I don't have to leave in disgrace. I'll research to get more information about the community's needs. I know that the local population speaks a language that would take me years to learn, even though I have a talent for languages. I will need an interpreter or two for French, Kikongo, and Lingala. That's not the least of the problems. There are cultural, religious, and social rules. Oh, my. Nothing is clear or straightforward."

"Mama Joyce, you'll grow used to how things move spiritually here," the short one said.

"Yes, okay. I'll keep collecting information to plan a project and get support." I was relieved and happy to have direction. They had to understand that my return would be for a project and not to live here. They looked at each other and said they understood what I was saying. My stomach growled from hunger. I thanked them and headed for the dining room.

***

Two evenings later, I stood to sneak off to the veranda after dinner. A delegation member followed me out of the room and asked, "Where do you go when you keep disappearing?"

I was reluctant to tell her. It would risk exposing my secret retreat and ending my private use of my precious place. "Oh, I hang around getting some air," I said, trying to minimize things, but she insisted I take her to see.

"Oh, this is lovely," she declared. Leaning on the cement banister, she looked over the valley below. "Those orange lights are cooking fires, right? They're like stars in earthly skies." Her attention then turned to the sky, and she asked. "Do you know anything about constellations?"

"I only remember the dippers and North Star. Why do you ask?"

"I was looking over there at that one. It seems to be in the wrong place."

"What do you mean?"

"My sister, bless her, was trying to teach me to identify some of them back home. Her favorite is Orion, and she taught me how to find it. Do you see those three bright stars?"

Staring upward, my gaze followed where she was pointing. "Yes. I see them."

"That's his belt. But I'm confused. The other stars aren't where I remember them in relation to it," she paused with a frown. "Anyway, like I said, I'm no expert. I'll ask my sister to see what she thinks. Maybe another time. Don't be surprised if you find me here from time to time. I'll bet your French-speaking friends showed you this place."

"No. I came across it while looking for a quiet place one day and asked if I could use it."

"I see. Well, I'll return or risk a search party," she said, slipping back into the house.

I sighed in relief and closed my eyes in thanks for peace. When I opened my eyes, I was startled to find one of the church officials standing beside me.

"So, what have you found out here alone?" he asked.

I laughed, replying, "I have found more questions each day and few answers."

"What is your question at this moment?"

"Well, one of my sisters just told me the positions of the constellations are out of order." I pointed to the three bright stars. "Like that one there."

"Yes," he nodded. "We have many visitors making the same comment. In Nkamba, all the constellations are viewable at all times. But it isn't those humanly created pictures that you should pay attention to. It is the signs and messages that God reveals to us through them." He swept his hand across the sky, drawing my attention from Orion to the Big Dipper.

"What does the Dipper mean?" I asked, but I saw no one there when I looked around.

I looked toward the doorway into the building. There was no sound and no one there. I shivered as goosebumps rose on my arms. Looking toward the sky again, a noise came behind me.

The delegation guide said from the doorway, "Mama Joyce, what are you doing out here alone in the dark?" He reached and switched on a light I didn't know existed.

"I was enjoying some quiet time," I said, hinting that company was unnecessary. He walked to stand beside me, either ignoring or missing the point. Looking up at his face, I saw something strange about the old scar on his forehead. "What caused those scars on your face?" I asked.

He said with a nervous chuckle, "When I was young, I had chicken pox. These are the scars from it. What made you ask?".

"A few minutes ago, one of the church officials came here."

"He did? It must have been an important moment. What did he say?"

I related to what had happened, from when the delegation member followed me until the church official disappeared. "It's funny, but I wonder if anyone has mentioned that the stars outlining the Big Dipper are in the same pattern as the scars on your forehead."

"What? No," he said with a stunned look. Then, looking at the Big Dipper, he cleared his throat and said, "Mama Joyce, you don't know the prophecy on my life. It says I'll be a big ladle, bringing many to this place. You just confirmed it. It's been sitting right in front of everyone on my face. No one ever made that connection, not even me. Why are you the one to see it?"

"I don't know. The church official pointed out the constellation and said what I told you."

He was silent for a long time, then swallowed hard. "In the evenings at home, my family sits together on the loft gazing at the sky. My favorite constellation is the Big Dipper. I knew there was a reason for this besides the beauty of God's handiwork, but I didn't know what."

"Did he send you out here?"

"No. I just felt the urge to find out where you were. This is tremendous. Thank you. I'm going to tell the church official," he said, hurrying away.

***

Near the end of our stay in Nkamba, the reporter in the delegation came to ask me to translate for a final interview with a church official. I knew my French was not up to translating, much less for an international American TV audience. She assured me the station's voiceover services would cover all mistakes. She needed to be sure the official understood all her questions and that she understood his responses, allowing her to ask further questions. I agreed to do it.

When I showed up at the interview, the official's grimace showed that he was not confident I could do the job. He asked if there was someone else to interpret. I don't know why he disdained me, but he sent his helper to find a more qualified interpreter.

I told him that that was fine if he did not want me to do this. I was his guest. I explained that I knew my language limitations but had agreed because I wanted to help the world understand God's mighty actions through the church. The reporter had assured me I wouldn't be heard or seen in the final product. With this information, he begrudgingly agreed to start. I prayed and did my best. By the session's end, he complimented my efforts and my French. The reporter and the official thanked me. I was overjoyed to make a concrete contribution to the mission after all. But there was more to come.

***

The delegation leader informed us that arrangements were being made for a possible audience with the new president when we returned to the capital city. If they were successful, we could ask only one approved question. I was happy with the question I was given to ask. "How would you ask us to pray for you in light of those saying you are too young for the job?" His answer was profound.

***

A few days later, there was a different meeting, which made me reflect deeply. It was with a woman who had been a young girl when she was a disciple of the church founder, Simon Kimbangu. One day, he was explaining what he saw in the future. He said African Americans would return to native African lands after the turn of the century. When listeners asked about this possibility, he named the area Kindolo, reserved for African Americans. This was the name of the city to be constructed for their return. He identified the little girl standing in their midst as confirmation of the prophecy. He said she would live to witness the prophecy fulfilled.

She was now elderly and wore a tired frown as I entered the room where she was waiting. Her daughter had brought her to the lodging center in Kinshasa because she wanted to meet the African Americans who had come.

The delegation leader called me to be introduced to this particular Kimbanguist disciple. She had met the famous disciple the prior year and warned that the disciple's vision was fading. The previous year, she had been surprised when the disciple had used her hands to feel her facial features. She wanted to do the same with me today. When I knelt before the disciple, she reached out and gently touched my face, her head nodding in recognition as her fingers gently traced my eye, nose, lips, and then my entire face. She repeated the process and sighed. I don't know if she met any of the other team members. She didn't appear to be sad or happy. She spoke to her daughter, who said her mother was tired and wanted to go home. With that, they left. At that moment, I was filled with a profound admiration for this historical figure, her resilience, and her unwavering faith.

I regret not capturing this moment with photographs or seizing the opportunity to ask the questions that swirled in my mind. How extraordinary it would have been to hear her testimony. Her life was shaped by her faith, courage, and commitment. She had made many sacrifices and endured pain. Finally, she had a family and was waiting for a prophecy to materialize. Since the tender age of ten, she had waited for decades to testify to a particular event.

It reminded me of the biblical story of Simeon in the temple. The Holy Spirit had revealed that he would not see death until he saw the Messiah. There was also the story of Anna, the prophetess who, at the same time as Simeon, testified that baby Jesus was the Messiah.

I would prepare for the next visit when she returned to meet the others. I wrote down my questions, but we left before her return. Soon after my arrival home, the sad news came that she had died. People speculated about who had released her by fulfilling the prophecy. She had been exhausted, but she was finally at rest. She had been privileged to know her focal life moment, which was the fulfillment of the prophecy. She had not let that future day prevent her from facing each day in the interim as a chance to do something meaningful.

Chapter 7

California

For almost a year, I had worked overtime, bent over backward, and struggled to find a compromise as a single mother and popular clinician to be both a good parent and medical provider. To be faithful to my work contract, I had endured physical and emotional challenges and financial hardships. So, it was frustrating when the administrators repeatedly gave unclear and nonspecific answers to my questions.

It would often anger me to think of the time and effort I had spent attending medical school and specialty training only to be forced to give my patients substandard care. The administrators, however, knowingly placed hurdles in the path of medical providers such as me that resulted in corporate gain. I felt this was deceptive and resisted their moves.

One day, an administrator came to my station with a direction for me to tell my patients what I considered a lie. It was the last straw. I gave my two-week notice. When I woke up that morning, the thought of resigning had not entered my mind. By deciding to leave, I was instantly sure of two things. First, I'd done my best to stay in my position by changing my office hours and working through lunches. I would advise anyone in this situation to do the same. Second, I already harbored regrets and wasn't willing to add another to the list. On a moral issue, I would not bend.

However, how would I meet my responsibilities for feeding my children, paying my mortgage and car payments, and all the associated insurance and bills? I needed a job without the same restrictions. The thought of working in a job with shifts came to mind. There would be no on-call nights or piles of medication refill requests.

After calling around, I found a job opening within an hour's distance from my house. When visiting the clinic, I was astonished to hear the terms. By working ten days a month, I would make the same amount as my last job without the deduction for partnership buy-in. God honored my stand for honesty. I was relieved that this job allowed me to spend time with my kids and participate in community activities.

Then, after a year of working shifts that were not chosen by more senior staff, I received a call from the competition. They offered me more pay, better hours, and a promotion. As clinic director, I would make the schedule, and they were closed on weekends. They said I was drawing clients away from them. This was a better offer, and I accepted. Things went well, and our patient volume increased. I engaged specialty consultants and more providers.

A colleague called, saying she was having conflicts with partners and wanted to know if there were any openings where I was. I recommended that she apply to the regional office. When she was sent for an interview, we agreed she was a good fit for the open afternoon shift position. After changing my schedule numerous times to adapt to her increasing frequency of "unforeseen events," I finally said that the schedule was made months in advance and should not have to be changed so often for one person, and the most recent request was refused.

I was shocked by a call from my regional director. This recently hired colleague had lied to the regional director to convince her to override my scheduling decision. I replied to the regional director's announcement. "When you offered me the job, one of the biggest attractions was that I would make the scheduling decisions. I don't think it was correct or wise to override my decision based solely on the word of a new person. In addition, you did so before seeking my input as the person's supervisor and clinic director. I feel your action was a betrayal of my trust. I also think it was a risk business-wise as well. You have the authority to do what you think best. However, these are not the descriptions of my duties and tasks in my contract when I came to work here. This person has shown their manipulative side before. I assure you it will not be the last time. If you had asked, I would have happily explained this to you. Now, I no longer trust you, and I want to find myself in the same situation in the future. For these reasons, I no longer wish to work here and will send you my two-week notice."

The regional director backpedaled, complimenting my excellent job making the clinic into a profit-making unit with happy staff, saying, "There's no need to leave over such a small issue."

I pointed out that everything she had just listed should have led to a consultation with me before she reversed my decision. Unfortunately, I disagreed this was a 'small' issue.

My previous job requested my return, and I thought I would. Before calling, I received an unexpected offer to head a medical group as part of a network of clinics based on Christian principles and focused on providing care for underserved communities. This offer tugged at my heartstrings.

I decided to sell my house since neither my children nor I planned to live in the city that had been our home for seven years. I gave away most of our furniture and appliances. It was strange to find I did not feel sad or empty. I felt light and satisfied. It was like fishing and struggling against the pull of a giant fish twisting and knotting its way around my fellow fishermen's lines. You "cut bait" or your fishing line, losing what was invested to prevent further loss.

I accepted and set out to a new location with a beautiful opportunity. But soon, frustration enveloped my new job, and layers of betrayal weighed on me. But how? Why was it wrong to ask for what was promised? This position offered opportunities for health education and mobile clinics through church groups, which I enjoyed. However, the guarantees made by the network did not materialize, leaving us disillusioned and disheartened.

Appointed as the initial group's lead doctor, my role was reduced to a messenger of the members' frustration to the network head. With my pleas ignored, I made an appointment and drove to his office to resign. Tears poured down my face, and my chest burned thinking about the things group members sacrificed to make this opportunity work. The network leadership had initially done considerable work before we joined but had recently become deaf to us. Two of us had already said they were withdrawing and planned to sue. The network was such a fantastic idea. Why was it dying?

An unknown number called my cell phone. A woman at my new church was calling to ask for help with overseas mission planning. Hearing of my experience with medical missions to Kenya, she wanted my input. This was so unexpected that it dispelled my anger. Her enthusiasm for missions was contagious and refreshing. I shared the need to plan with the local providers and mentally prepare the team for the shock of an overseas environment. We agreed to meet on Sunday after church. I had reached my destination and parked the car as we continued to discuss. She stopped suddenly and asked where I was at the moment. I told her I was on my way to resign. When she asked why, a flood door opened, and I poured out my heart to her with buckets of tears.

"May I share with you what the Spirit has dropped in my heart?" she asked.

"Sure," I said, wiping my tears. I walked into the building and entered the elevator.

"Don't resign today. Go into that office with your eyes and ears open. You'll be surprised at what God has prepared for you. Do you understand?" she asked.

"Even if I don't understand why, I understand what I am to do."

"Good. Where are you now?"

"I am at the office door."

"Go on in. God has gone before you. Call me when you're done. I am praying for you."

"Thank you," I said, turning off my phone and entering.

"He's finishing up with a patient," the receptionist said. She looked up and frowned, then quickly stood to open the hall door. "Let me take you to the conference room."

Wondering what had made her frown when she saw my face, I waited until she left and placed my things on the table to mark my impending return. I hurried to the bathroom we had passed in the hallway. Gazing in shock at my reflection in the mirror, I understood her reaction. My eyes were red and swollen from crying, and my makeup had run and smeared. I looked insane with out-of-control emotions. Had I walked in as angry as I had been before I talked to the missionary moments ago, she probably would have been afraid enough to call the police.

I washed my face and practiced smiling at my reflection. Hadn't I been told that God had gone before me? He had prepared something for me, so I took a deep breath and returned to the conference room. I continued praying, happy that someone else was also praying for me.

The network head hurried into the room a few minutes later, clutching some papers. He took a deep breath, his hands trembling as he tried to smooth the pages. He stopped his advance toward the table, avoiding eye contact, and took another deep breath. I thought my appearance or the receptionist's report of my appearance might have unsettled him. Realizing he had not looked at my face, I opened my mouth to greet him.

He held his palm toward me to stop and said, "Before you say anything, I wanted to tell you about my experience on the plane yesterday. I was trying to take an inflight nap but was jolted awake when I heard a voice say, 'What do you think you are doing? Joyce is my daughter. You are trying to put my square daughter in a round hole of your making. Let me show you what I have called her to do.' I took out my computer and typed what I was told. This is it," he said, sitting across from me and handing me the papers. "I know you want to resign. I've seen your frustration. If I arrange to let you accomplish those things written there, will you stay?"

I took the papers and curiously began to read. I was astounded as each line resonated with my heart. I smiled at him. "If you arrange to let me do these things, I will stay."

"Good," he said with a sigh of relief and stood. "We will talk about the details later."

"When?" I asked.

"I have patients to see for the rest of the afternoon. I will call you this evening."

Smiling, I hurried to the car and called my new missionary friend. Without saying hello, she answered on the first ring. "I'm singing hallelujah in my spirit" were her opening words.

I told her the details and read some of the descriptions. "I can't believe it. It's a miracle."

"Wow. Look at our God. This man is afraid, but his heart hasn't changed. Let God take care of him. You pray and prepare yourself to live what God has confirmed to you. Maybe we'll even travel together soon. At least we'll both go on a mission. Let's pray for God's guidance. We'll talk on Sunday." She prayed, and my heart filled with hope and joy.

The network head did not call that evening or reply to my call for weeks afterward. However, he did schedule an annual physical exam, which showed my blood pressure was elevated. His intervention and a cardiologist referral were both God-sent. Adverse events from high blood pressure plagued both sides of my family. It's confusing in circumstances like this to categorize someone as good or bad. I am so glad God keeps that responsibility for himself. Only He can see a person's heart and judge it. I was grateful for his attention to my health.

Chapter 8

A call one evening from a colleague in distress opened an unexpected door. She wanted me to take her place on a medical mission to the Democratic Republic of the Congo. Weeks prior, she had promised to go there as a medical professional. That morning, she had been notified of a crucial interview for a highly desired position that would take place during the scheduled mission time. She did not want to leave the mission stranded, so she thought I might be an excellent substitute. Happy to be able to do something worthwhile, I agreed to go for two weeks.

Delighted that she could hand the responsibility over to me, she said she would call the mission leader and give her my number. "If all goes well, she will call you tonight or tomorrow. Thank you. I was dreading having to make the call to pull out. You are a lifesaver."

"This may be just what I need. I'm glad to help and look forward to the call."

I needed to notify the network head, but there was no response to my several calls. This meant going in person for a face-to-face exchange—a meeting I did not look forward to. There would probably be resistance to my taking earned vacation time off. On the other hand, he seemed to have forgotten the sheets he had given me and his promise to call.

When I arrived at the primary office, I saw his car there. I parked nearby, went inside, and was unexpectedly ushered into the conference room.

He rushed into the room minutes later. "Isn't it funny? I was planning to call you this evening. I'm glad you came by. Forgive me for being so busy." He sat on the edge of his seat.

"I've come to tell you I will be leaving on a medical mission to the DRC."

"A mission? So, you'll be coming back?'

"Yes. I'll return in two weeks. After that, I'm not sure where I'll go. You haven't kept your word, and I don't expect you to. But I'll give notice before I leave permanently," I said.

"When you come back, you'll see a big change. I've already made some progress," he said, leaning back in the chair. "So, when are you coming back?"

"I will send you my vacation dates once they are confirmed."

"Yes, that would be good. Thank you for letting me know. I've been busy looking at alternatives, and I'll soon have time to discuss the next steps with the group."

I left hoping the mission would be enough time to clear my head and put me on the right track when I returned. All that was needed now were trip details.

The mission leader called for me to meet with her. I agreed, excited and eager to learn more about the details and what equipment we needed to bring. Although the discussion was somewhat undetailed, having travel dates and information about the country was good.

She explained that this was a memorable season for the church hosting our group, the Kimbanguist Church. Delegations from all over the world will be attending. The church was the world's largest indigenous African church. It had the distinction of having the only all-Black symphony orchestra worldwide. The church was apolitical but very influential. As the American delegation leader, she would carry a lot of responsibility and expected full cooperation from each team member. The country's president was the son of the recently assassinated former president. He was young and had taken the post to prevent a civil war. Things had become peaceful.

The data showed that citizens in many countries were impoverished despite their countries having vast natural wealth in oil and precious minerals. They lived in squalor and were deprived of effective healthcare systems. Having led similar outreaches in Kenya for years, I knew that the local medical providers were experts in assessing how to make the most of the available resources and what would fulfill the present needs. We usually beta-tested rapid test kits to determine the mode of treatment or refer patients for further care.

Unlike those trips, this time, I knew none of the other team members, the parts of the country to be visited, the resources being taken, or the mission plan. The strong sense of direction I usually experienced when going on a medical mission was absent. It felt like I had been blindfolded, twirled around, and given a stick to swing at a piñata suspended in the area in front of me. Was I running from my lousy situation more than running to a solution? My dad had this saying: "If you only focused on what you were running from, you might end up somewhere worse." Not wanting the aversion of my present situation to blind me made me more apprehensive and prayerful. I hoped it would give me the energy and courage to release all of the goodies in the piñata ahead of me on my life's path.

I remained uneasy about the continued lack of information and communication with the other team members. It was also unclear if other medical personnel would be involved. Did the mission leader have a system for recording information? How would we transfer prescription information to the mobile pharmacy? Did she want me to bring any medication with me?

I had a dream that comforted me. I was wearing one of my favorite black evening dresses. My hair was freshly done, and unusually for me, I was wearing full makeup and acrylic nails. I looked like I was going to a gala. My doorbell rang. When I opened it, no one was visible, but a voice said, "Are you ready?"

"Yes, of course," I replied, closing the door behind me. "Where are we going? I asked.

"You will see. For now, I want you to take a step forward."

"A step? One step?" I questioned.

"Yes, one step."

I stepped forward and said, "Okay, now what?" Looking around, I saw that we were now surrounded by sweltering sand.

The voice distracted my attention. "Now I want you to jump over that crevasse."

"Crevasse?" I asked and noticed an opening in the ground ahead of me. It was not wider than two feet but extended in both directions as far as I could see. I would not be able to continue the journey without crossing it. Walking up to the edge and looking down inside, I heard the sounds of a rapidly flowing river at a great depth. Nothing was visible. While the width was not great, I was wearing heels, putting me at a disadvantage. This made me hesitate and reassess what I was about to do. "I will need to back up and get a running start to be sure I land safely," I assessed.

"If you wish. Do what you think is necessary. You need to get to the other side."

With a running start, I cleared the gaping hole. "Done," I said, smoothing my dress.

"Next, I want you to climb that mountain."

Out of nowhere, a few feet away, there appeared a mountain. "Where did that come from?"

"You must climb to the top."

"But if the goal is to arrive at the other side, it would be easier to go around the base."

"No, you must climb to the top."

"But my outfit will be ruined."

"It's okay. I'll take care of that. You climb," the voice reassured.

As I climbed, I broke out in a light sweat. One of my high heels broke off. I removed both shoes and threw them to the side. Before long, runs began making their way along my stockings. "I'd be sad at the summit if I were told to descend the other side," I whined.

"Keep climbing."

Frustration increased as my hair came loose and fell over my face and ears. My makeup showed in a long smear on the back of my hands as I wiped the sweat beading on my forehead and trickling down my face. Feeling the cold sweat marks under my arms, I climbed, finally reaching the top. A refreshing breeze blew gently, and all signs of sweat resolved. The view was nothing short of perfect natural beauty, inspiring spiritual awe. From the serene mountain peak, the lush, fruitful green valley and pasture stretched to the horizon. A deep, inexplicable peace and sense of satisfaction engulfed me. I sat on the ground, my dress no longer a consideration.

"This is wonderful," I sighed. "I'm so glad I made the effort. Can I stay?"

"No," came the response.

"Please don't tell me to go down the backside," I pleaded as my eyes widened.

"No," was the quiet response. "I want you to jump to the next mountain."

"What?" I exclaimed, my brow wrinkled in confusion. Looking around, I saw no visible mountains. I shook my head vigorously, asking myself why I was looking for mountains. No one hops along mountaintops. "Look. The other things were doable, but that's impossible."

"Impossible is an interesting thought. Do you remember the step I asked you to take? Look at that tract of land. There was a wide span of wetland. That is the extent of that step."

"What, one step? That's not possible. Okay. What about the crevasse?"

"Do you see that?" He pointed to a vast canyon with a river running along the bottom.

I fell onto my back, looking up into the cloudless sky. "So, you did all of that?" I realized aloud humbly. "I didn't do anything. None of it was possible."

"When you obey, I can do things beyond your imagination."

I closed my eyes and considered the immensity of what I had just understood. Finally, I asked, "So, if I close my eyes and jump, you will make me land on another mountaintop?"

"Yes."

"Okay, then," I said and jumped to my feet. Crouching, I closed my eyes and prepared to run and jump as high as possible.

"Wait, not now. I will tell you when."

I awoke in bed, arms bent, head poised to jump, waiting to hear "Now."

"Lord, I don't know if this is the step, the jump, or the mountaintop already. Help me to be obedient and willing to hear," I prayed. "I want to trust you. Your view is more complete than any I could ever have. But it is hard to walk confidently when I don't see the path clearly before me. You will have to help me."

An image flashed before me. Two people were walking with their elbows linked, happily talking. They stopped when a bicycle whirred across their path, narrowly missing colliding with them. One of them had seen the bike approaching and stopped immediately. With eyes blankly looking forward, the other was kept from the danger of proceeding by her linked arm. At this point, I realized one was blind and the other sighted. A frown appeared across the forehead of the blind person as questions were asked and answered. The sighted person then told the blind person it was ok to continue. The danger had passed. The blind person smiled, and they resumed their walk.

Yes, I thought. *That's exactly how it should be.* "Lord, help me to stick close to you and not depend on what I think lies ahead of me but confidently on what I know you see."

Chapter 9

When I returned to the US, it should have been no surprise to find the network medical group was in splinters. It was time to search for a new job. Conveniently, my brother owned a nearby clinic and was having staffing problems. He allowed me to stay at his house while I worked for him when he went on vacation, and I did short vacation relief for other doctors as I shuttled back and forth between Northern and Southern California.

In the meantime, I searched for ways to fund a project in the DRC. I visited the delegation guide and became close to his lovely family. One morning, I visited them unannounced on my way to Southern California. When I arrived, he said he wanted to call the DRC because of the news he had heard about the recent death of Papa. After a while, he started staring at me and said, "Yes, she is here." He held the cell phone toward me and said, "This is the church's new head. He wants to speak to you."

I took the phone and heard him say, "Mama Joyce. When are you coming to live here?"

My heart skipped a beat when he said his father's exact words. "We are waiting for you."

As I started to give all kinds of excuses, I was struck as if by a bolt of lightning with the memory of the list I had given the previous church head. They had all been dealt with one by one until all were resolved. Why would I start a new list? Deeply convicted, I answered, "I will try to come as soon as possible."

I had learned a secret from the Kimbanguist Church. The word "impossible" did not stand in their way. It gave them a chance to see the impossible birthed into existence. They had built the largest church on the continent by hand. Buckets of soil had been passed upward until the massive hole for the foundation was dug. Buckets of cement had then been passed down until the foundation was poured. This had been followed by buckets of cement being passed upward to build the walls.

Then there was the orchestra, which sounded so professional, consisting of inexperienced youngsters directed by a maestro without a background in orchestra management. They were also the first African-based church accepted into the World Council of Churches. So many other impossible accomplishments had started with the statement I had come to love: "Yes, it is impossible. But what would be our first step if we could do it?" From there, they would march step by step toward another miracle.

The church's unity was shown through its practice of giving offerings. Whatever they had—groceries, gifts, or cash—was given to compete in fundraising sessions. Sometimes, these competitions would occur between women and men or music groups. Seeing their joy as they passed was quite a sight, with the losers promising to win the next time.

But I delayed my departure as I grappled with sadness. How sad the sick people and orphans would be to think I had abandoned them by stopping the Kenyan annual medical mission. Then again, there was the frightening idea of having no salary to do anything.

There was also the distraction of my medical association. I had risen, for various reasons, from state to national-level elected positions. Not having sought this, I had had delegations or individuals sent to test my willingness to run for office. The thought was attractive because I had many ideas to lead our organization toward international partnerships to address worldwide health issues. I could not do all three things. Two of them would have to be abandoned. Was I abandoning my Black medical colleagues across the nation to go work in rural DRC?

Like many things, having conflicting choices is not always what it seems. While emotional, financial, or political factors are used to apply pressure, the only crucial factor that pushes us in the right direction is the God factor. It just doesn't always look like it at first.

There were different things to fret about for days on end. One afternoon after work, I sat fretting on my bed, leaning against the headboard. The wall I was facing opened like a massive window to the horizon. I felt a breeze blowing and saw a man in the distance, flying across the sky like Superman. He was African and dressed in a simple white robe style from decades ago. He changed his trajectory and flew toward me.

Concern rising, I asked, "What are you doing?".

"*I* am coming for you," was his reply.

This got my attention. In fear, I sat bolt upright. "Why?" I asked, "What have I done?"

"I am **coming** for you," he said again with a different word emphasis. As the figure drew nearer, I wondered if he was the death angel. However, something was familiar and kind about him, like he was from the church in the DRC.

"I said I would come," I said, closing my eyes, not believing what I saw. When I opened my eyes, the tall man stood at the foot of my bed, arms outstretched toward me.

"I am coming for *you*," he said.

"I will come," I pleaded loudly. "But I want to go in an airplane. I don't want you to carry me there." My heart raced, fearing he would scoop me up and take me back to the DRC. This was real. I was terrified, unable to take deep breaths.

He smiled and nodded, letting his arms drop. I sighed deeply in relief, leaning back against the headboard as I closed my eyes. When I opened my eyes again, he had disappeared, but I wasn't sure he had left the room. My wall remained open to the distant sky with a slight breeze. So, I kneeled to check under the bed and then in the closet. The wall then closed abruptly, and it seemed everything was back to normal.

My sister-in-law called downstairs, "Are you okay? Was that you or the TV?"

"I'm okay," I replied. Then, under my breath, "I've got to make travel plans."

I told my mom and siblings I planned to go to the DRC for a while. But first, I needed to put a formal end to the annual medical missions to Kenya. We made our last Kenyan mission trip. It was sad as we explained it was our last and said goodbye. I also took my mom on a side flight to the DRC during this trip. I wanted her to meet the people and the church officials. She was treated with high respect by the church in Kinshasa. When we visited Nkamba, the church headquarters, and the church head, she turned to me and said, "So, you have found your tribe."

My heart was so happy that she had no reservations about my intentions to make an extended stay. For reasons I cannot explain, I returned to the US and didn't make immediate travel plans. My three children were concerned. They had all been born in Kenya but had grown up in California. They were all adults and did not spend much time with me, but the thought of me being so far out of reach in an unstable country, in an area with no cell phone access, made them understandably uneasy.

The way to settle this was to take them to see the place and meet the people where I would be staying. I booked tickets for all of us to fly to the DRC during the school holiday to meet the same people who had calmed my mother's concerns. They planned to see where I would stay and leave me there while they returned to their lives and school.

We stayed in the first house built for the returning African Americans in the separate village called Kindolo. Nothing less than luxurious, it had two bedrooms, a modern kitchen, an expansive bathroom with beautiful tiling, a dining room, and a living room. It had handcrafted furnishings and a stunning countryside view. Hearing that the former church head, Papa, had come and spent some afternoons in the house praying, I felt it was a blessed place.

The new church head met with me and asked why I had come to live in Nkamba. This seemed strange since he had said they were waiting for me, but I told him of my promise to the previous church head. For the first time, I shared my vision of the man flying from the DRC to get me. He asked if I understood the man had brought me a heavenly message.

The church head then spoke to my children privately. They reported later that he had promised and assured them I would be well cared for. This tipped the scale, convincing them to be more at ease about my plan to stay. Their visit was over too soon. They mainly seemed at peace with my decision to stay when they left. We returned to Kinshasa for their departure. I cried once they boarded the plane. When the plane took off, I was left in Kinshasa without a clear direction. What was it exactly that I was supposed to do?

The answer came when someone decided the day to return to Nkamba arrived. The car stopped on the main road for fuel. I was seated in the front passenger seat with three church heavy hitters, including the guide for the first delegation, now my friend. What lay ahead of me? Anxious, I started to pray silently and heard a clear voice say, "Now." I turned to see who had spoken. The guide sat with his eyes closed. The other two men had gotten out for some reason.

A thought flashed across my mind, lighting a memory of standing on a mountaintop. *It was the word I was waiting to hear.* I had stood braced to jump to the next mountaintop for a long time. Excited, I closed my eyes and leaned forward, with my arm bent to help thrust me as far as possible. I jumped forward, lifted myself off the seat, and then plopped down, shaking the car.

"What are you doing, Mama Joyce?" the delegation guide asked, "What's happening?"

I told him the story of the dream and then the command I'd heard a few minutes before.

"This is big. Why didn't you ever tell me this?"

"I didn't think about it. I'd almost forgotten."

"This is big," he repeated, looking around the car. "Wait, where are the others? I must tell them." He got out to search for them. They returned, I retold the story, and we discussed its meaning. What was the next mountain? Were there other mountains? I had no answers.

Chapter 10

The Democratic Republic of the Congo

Upon returning to Nkamba, I directed the clinic near the church headquarters. It was incredible that I had not visited the clinic before. The building seemed large. I soon understood the term "clinic" was used for any place where healthcare was provided. That could be an outpatient clinic or a small hospital. This site had both. It was the only health center within sixteen miles.

Footpaths and dirt roads connected the surrounding communities, and most people traveled on foot. There were over two dozen villages in the area, and the church welcomed a regular influx of visitors from all over the world. While miracles occurred daily on the premises of the church headquarters, the clinic addressed regular medically treatable cases. It arranged for patients with severe diseases who did not believe in miraculous cures to be transferred to a government hospital.

A head nurse had run the clinic for a few years before my arrival. When we met, he made no eye contact and did not smile when he limply shook my hand. I didn't understand his singular unhappiness and cold welcome. He seemed to try to discourage me by explaining that unpaid staff members served the clinic. He explained they remained because there was a decent place to stay in the employee quarters on the grounds. The head nurse then gave me a tour, explaining that the clinic was not profitable. There were two significant reasons for this, according to him. First, there had never been a doctor stationed there, which was required for it to be designated a hospital and receive government supplies. Second, the church referred many patients to the clinic for care. They arrived with a coupon from the head of the church as his commitment to pay the bill. The head nurse reported this payment was slow if it came at all. The surrounding local population was unable to pay cash for medical care. I thought resolving these two issues would make him happy. So, I focused on them and added one of my own to the list.

Patients in the hospital were given a thin foam mattress. They brought their mattress covering. Their relatives or messengers went to buy medication and food for them. Any money they gave the hospital was seen as a tip for cleaning the floors and providing drinking water. This money went to the head nurse and was divided among the employees. If the patient had no relative to live at the hospital to fetch water, bathe, or cook for them, they suffered in addition to their illness. Few had money to pay someone to help them.

When I spoke to the church head, he promised to send payments regularly for the church-sponsored patients. He also permitted us to plant a vegetable garden down the slope behind the clinic on land by the stream.

God had given me the idea to provide access to the community by letting village youths work in the garden. They would earn a set cash equivalent per square yard to clear, weed, plant, or water. The credit would be awarded for completely tending to a specific land surface, not for the time spent. This same opportunity was offered to patients' family members. This cash equivalent would build a fund to pay for the hospitalization and medicine for their fellow villagers and family members. They could also purchase mosquito nets to reduce malaria cases. The young people earned respect and appreciation by productively using the time they would have wasted. It was an opportunity for family members to help after visiting someone hospitalized.

We made sure to present our first harvest to the church head. He said we had provided food to feed a delegation that had arrived when there was nothing in the pantry.

The sale of the produced vegetables brought in money to provide the employees with sugar, milk, salt, and tea. We could grow vegetables to give as part of the employees' salaries. There was also money to buy the necessary clinic supplies and medications. We planned to sell the produced vegetables at the local market, increasing access to healthy food for those around us. We could also sell the extra produce to the wagons that came around purchasing produce from farmers. Our clinic was not only self-sustaining but also contributed to the surrounding community's health.

Based on my belief in the significant impact of health awareness, permission was granted for another request to run classes for women's health. For the first class, we invited one representative from each of the twenty-six villages surrounding the clinic. We set up the room with thirty chairs facing a movable blackboard. It soon appeared that was not going to suffice.

I watched with growing anxiety as hundreds of women streamed into the hospital compound. They filled the dedicated room, sitting on the floor when all the chairs or stools were taken. Those unable to find space inside demanded that the windows be opened to allow them to hear while standing outside. Women had come with babies tied to their backs. Others stepped slowly with canes. The head nurse, who would translate my words, had told me beforehand to let the head village women control the running of the meeting. Despite there being so many women, these leaders kept remarkable order.

At the end of the class, I explained that we were not equipped to have so many women attending at once. I suggested they have a village representative attend the classes. That representative could relay the information in sessions in the villages, saving them all time and effort. Murmurs erupted as soon as the nurse translated my suggestion.

The head nurse warned, "They are not pleased with your suggestion that fewer come."

In the beginning, the most prominent seat had been left empty. The woman occupying that priority chair conferred with others in the front row. She then stood and said, "Thank you for your suggestion. But we want you to come to the villages to give the classes. We have heard beneficial things today. We have taken notes but do not know enough to teach the others."

Applause thundered in her support as the head nurse bent near me to give me the translation. Then he added, "If you spend that much time in the villages, you will not be able to treat the hospitalized. You must refuse this request."

"I agree, but we must offer another solution. Ask her if they would accept us providing sheets with information to take back and a binder to keep them in. Anyone could consult the sheets or ask questions, and the representative could refer to them."

Applause erupted again as the head nurse translated this.

The lead woman consulted with the women in the front row. She smiled and said, "If you cannot come, give the representatives the written information of what was taught to take back with them."

The head nurse translated the lead woman's words. "It appears you have a deal. So, I will translate and type out the information for next month's meeting. I will need time off to do this."

Chapter 11

My home was the only house in the new village occupied full-time. Wanting it to be an example, I changed the yard to make it look more personal. Flowers were planted as borders around a thinned front lawn. Standing on the hilltop in the gentle breeze in the early morning and at the end of the workday was comforting. It reminded me of the many times, as a child, I would climb the hill behind our house away from the clamor below and sit there reveling in the same kind of gentle hilltop breeze rustling the fields of dried grass. At night, the houses were alive with squeaks and scratchy bat movements. From experience, I knew that with time, the stench and stains of bat excrement would fill the ceilings with a horrible odor. My request that lights be placed along the open attic edge of the roof was thought to be out of fear of bats, but it was to deter them from destroying the attic space. This was a special house, and it deserved effort to preserve it.

I was allowed to use the hollow behind the house to plant corn and vegetable seeds but not to erect a protective fence. Unfortunately, neighbors' animal herds were allowed to graze on the field blanketed in green shoots several times despite my complaints. I thought it was done purposefully at times as I watched the shepherd stand idly, letting the animals run onto the field. There was no help given to me in shooing them away. I knew no effort had been made to keep them away when I wasn't there. It wasn't surprising when I was told at harvest that the corn seeds from America had not given good results. It was not worth my giving any further explanation.

While preparing to go to work one morning, my driver arrived early with a message. The church head wanted me to come by the residence before leaving for the clinic. This was highly unusual. As we drove, we could not imagine the possible reason for the same. When we arrived, the church head was seated, praying for people who had formed a long line beside him. He made no sign for me to approach, so I took a place with the officials and staff behind him and waited.

A man kneeled before him, and the church head called me after they talked. When I approached, he said, "This man has come from very far, asking for healing from his incurable disease." I listened, waiting for him to continue. Then he said, "Mama Joyce, you should take him to the hospital. This is a case for you."

A case for me? I was shocked, unable to say anything, as thoughts ran through my mind. *How could this be a case for me? What was wrong with the man? Why did the church head not just pray for him?* The man had not found medical relief at home, having come from a distance.

He gasped and cried when he heard what the church head said. I had to wait for the interpretation, so there was a lag. He was frantically backing away from me and begging the church head to pray for him. I asked myself why as well. The church head motioned for people to assist the man in getting to my car. With pursed lips, the man shook off their hands and walked over to my car, where my driver opened the door for him to climb in. With stiff shoulders, he sat, refusing to look at me. I sympathized with him and thought of all kinds of excuses for his rude behavior. He was probably feeling embarrassed after being refused prayer for healing. Coming from a rural area with few female professionals, he may have thought he was being sent to be cared for by an unqualified woman. He had most likely already tried medical remedies. I prayed that when I knew his diagnosis, a way to help him would be revealed to me. When we arrived at the clinic, I called the staff to help the man get inside and ready to be examined. I went to drop things off at my office.

I learned later that the head nurse had come to see what all the excitement was about when I arrived. Somehow, this event crossed a red line in the nurse's mind. Perhaps he was tired of being second in charge or left out of the loop. Hearing what had just happened, he instructed the staff to take the patient to a bed, where he performed an exam. He then told the staff that the church head had meant for me to transport the patient so that he could care for him. He stated that I was mistaken in thinking I was supposed to manage the care. He ordered medication to be brought to the bedside.

As I neared, the caregiver encountered me in the corridor. She informed me of what had happened. She explained that they knew what the head nurse said was not true. He had not been there when the church head had called and spoken to me. Nor had any message had been sent to him. His attitude showed he wanted to prove his superiority by being able to report to the church head that he had treated and cured the man. However, they dared not obey his orders and risk losing their jobs. I thanked her for the information and rapidly went to see the patient.

When I arrived, the head nurse was explaining his planned treatment to the new patient. The caregiver quietly placed the topical medication ordered by the head nurse at the bedside. I went to stand between the head nurse and the patient and asked for the story of the problem and to see the area involved.

As the patient begrudgingly told his story, the caregiver translated it to me. The head nurse interrupted to say all this had already been done, and the treatment had been ordered. The man refused to lift the cloth covering him to allow my examination. He said he wanted the head nurse to treat him. He had already done an exam. After a reminder of what the church head had said, he relented, but his narrowed eyes and clenched jaw spoke of his inner rebellious thoughts.

It was understandable why the man did not want me to see his problem as he lifted the cloth. An extensive fungal infection of the skin covering the area from his lower abdomen to his upper thighs. A bacterial infection had developed over the weeping red and swollen surface, worsened by the patient's scratching. The fungal stench was nauseating, and I struggled to keep a placid expression. While relieved it was not cancer, he faced a pretty dangerous situation.

I explained to the patient that we had to immediately get this bacterial infection under control to prevent it from becoming a more severe and possibly fatal blood infection. The regimen had to be a carefully managed combination of medicines. I gave the orders for topical, oral, and IV medications. The head nurse reached out to stop the caregiver from following my orders. I asked why. The head nurse smirked in front of all the patients and other nurses, and after turning to make sure everyone was listening, he asked me, "Do you know the diagnosis and the correct treatment?" He then explained how he had planned to treat it and showed me the medications he had ordered, trying to humiliate me.

The patient said he wanted the head nurse to care for him using his medication. However, I knew effective medical care for him was both crucial and urgent.

Usually, to save the head nurse embarrassment, I would have taken him aside, explained the situation's urgency, and shown him the medical books with the recommended treatment. I would have told him of the two times I had seen this in advanced stages that had required surgery and a lengthy, nearly fatal hospitalization. Unfortunately, he had removed these options. My heart was pounding as we were surrounded by complete, motionless silence.

My answer was given in a measured tone: "I most certainly know the diagnosis, the nature of both infections present, and the probability for them rapidly getting worse. The exact methods of treatment are well known to me. It will require more than you have prescribed because you have completely neglected to treat one infection." I cleared my throat. "It is my goal that he leave here alive. As you are perfectly aware, this is my patient, given directly by the church head because he thought I would treat him correctly."

The head nurse snidely said, "I have more experience than you."

I added a warning. "I will report you to the church head if you dare to change or add anything to my orders. Please move out of the way and let the caregiver pass."

The head nurse stuck his chin out and stormed away without another word. The caregiver ran to prepare what I had ordered, removing the tray of medication ordered by the head nurse. This was not a battle of my choosing. The only victory would be the patient's recovery.

The man had visibly improved in three days. On the seventh day, the swelling and oozing of the bacteria-infected part were resolved. He asked the caregiver to translate his gratitude to me and explained that when he had come to ask for prayer from the church head, he had thought he had cancer. The problem had lasted for so long and spread no matter what medication he was given. Anger had consumed him when the church head had told him to let me treat him. He had felt like he was being discarded. Now, he was sorry for being disrespectful and not understanding. He promised to pray for God's blessing on me for the rest of his life. I had given him the correct medicine and respect despite his bad behavior. He felt much better and wanted to go home.

I asked him to wait three more days in the holy city and then take the medication home to complete the treatment. I gave him instructions for further care and to present himself to the church head before he left. The head nurse said he was needed at home for a sick family member. He left before the patient presented himself to the church head and remained away for a long time.

***

We had little access to supplies unless we drove to Kinshasa. Hearing that some free supplies were available, I visited some international nonprofit offices to see if we could get what we needed. We received free packages of mosquito nets with a promise of more. Because many people in our area repeatedly became ill from malaria, and babies died, I was thrilled. The head nurse had returned and appeared to have a much better attitude. My joy was stifled when he said people would refuse to use them. They were afraid because they were told there was poison in the net to kill mosquitos. They thought it could also kill them or make them sick. He said I had wasted my time and efforts.

With my belief rising, I knew there must be a way to show people the nets' benefits. If I tried to convince them individually, they might feel they were betraying the community's wisdom and risking being ostracized. They must be convinced to use the nets based on a shared experience. However, there was no way to make an engaging video or commercial with people who resembled and spoke like them.

I had an idea and asked permission to present a skit the following Saturday.

Two animated local women agreed to help me by playing mothers with babies. One bought a net and let her baby sleep under the net with her. The other did not. I played the buzzing giant mosquito who was unhindered to bite the unprotected baby who went on to have a severe case of malaria. The mother, who slept under the net, was malaria-free and played with her happy, healthy baby. Acting like a frustrated mosquito blocked by the net, I mimicked being unable to get through to them. The audience hissed at me. When I faked becoming weak and finally falling dead outside the net, people roared with laughter and cheers.

I knew we had success when a woman in the audience yelled to the sick baby's mother, "Mama, you better buy a net if you don't want your baby to die."

Another woman yelled, "Here's my money. That net just killed a strong American mosquito. That's what I want."

Everyone laughed and applauded as I stood and bowed with our makeshift drama team. After the meeting, we ran out of net supplies. People teased me for weeks and made buzzing sounds when I came near. The message had been successfully relayed. Progress was being made.

***

I did not stay outside in the evenings unless it was a special event. One such event occurred when we hosted a visitor who could help us get a healthcare grant from the US. We visited the church's holdings, including a weather station on an open hilltop.

During the data collection demonstration, I continuously swatted mosquitos. Ultimately, I ran to sit in the car, having sustained several large bites on my arms and legs.

We also asked a malaria research team to visit our area. We were glad to be included in the study. They planned to bring a supply of tests and treatment for school children. What was not used would be left to test and treat those students absent at the clinic. The research was to be done in the nearby schools to test and then treat those who tested positive. They could not give an exact arrival date, but it would be within the next thirty days.

The research team arrived on the day of the second women's class. It was terrible timing, I thought. Running the women's class prevented me from being with the school team.

We set up the classroom as before, confident of a reasonable crowd this time. The papers had been printed, and we waited. Again, hundreds came to the class. The number was fewer than the first time, but it still filled the area surrounding the building. I wasn't feeling well after a restless night of preparation. I thought we would get by with the head nurse yelling the translation. The women in the front row insisted that the women outside wanted to hear my voice even if they could not understand my words. My head started throbbing as my throat became sore. It was the most terrible headache of my life. Having to yell at the crowd while missing school visits was enough to provoke and worsen the throbbing in my head. My driver, a nurse by training, eyed me with concern. He was always overprotective of me. I refused when he wanted to test me for malaria.

I had never had malaria while living in Kenya or traveling around Africa, so I assumed an immune factor or something protected me. We met that afternoon at the residence to hear the malaria research team's rapid report. It was surprising to hear that so many asymptomatic children had tested positive for malaria. The team wanted to leave after the report because they planned to continue their testing in another city in the morning. They explained that they had made unexpected progress in our schools. If they drove that night and started early in the morning, they could be in Kinshasa before nightfall. They left open boxes of testing materials and medication to allow testing for the children absent from school that day or others.

Waving goodbye to them in the plaza took the last of my strength. I waited inside the Hall of Honor for my driver to pack the malaria supplies and bring the car around the front.

The church head passed me and asked, "Doctor, are you tired or sick?"

"I'm tired, I think." Leaning on the sofa to rest my increasingly heavy throbbing head.

"No. You are sick," he looked around. "Where is your driver?"

"He's coming,"

"Good, you need to go home to Kindolo."

A few minutes later, I arrived at my house, exhausted. The smell of dinner sickened me, so I announced my intention to go straight to bed. The driver insisted on a malaria test again, so I agreed, knowing this was the only way to make him leave me alone. I was happy the test was negative. He wasn't satisfied and said he would retest in three hours. When he returned, I was almost too weak to walk. This time, the test was strongly positive. He insisted on seeing me take the first treatment dose and gave my live-in housekeeper overnight care instructions.

The following three days were a blur to me. Later, they told me about raging fevers and nightmares that made me scream out in my sleep. Severe nausea persisted, making it impossible to eat. The driver/nurse secured a more potent medication. Tests showed severe anemia, the result of a type of malaria often resulting in death. He was permitted to take me to Kinshasa in case a transfusion was needed. The new drug was effective, and I started eating and taking iron tablets. I was weak for a long time but thankful that God had used this driver/nurse to save my life.

I was more determined than ever to improve the community's general health. My research showed that the DRC government hospitals received significant supplies and benefits. We wanted to apply for hospital status, but the Ministry of Health required me to get a Tropical Disease Certificate. I would spend months in Kinshasa, rotating through several university hospital departments. This had to be completed before the hospital application could be processed. I would have to leave Nkamba to live in Kinshasa. I would move to the church center to lodge in an apartment, where I had stayed during my first visit to Kinshasa. I thought six months was not such a long time, and I headed to Kinshasa in high spirits.

Chapter 12

One consistent thread throughout my life is the belief that God has called me to follow Him. At nine, I decided to answer that call during a Sunday School class. The teacher told the story of God's indescribably immense love for me. The knowledge that He loves me, despite all my failures and wrong choices, left me overwhelmed then, and it still does today.

I was convinced I was supposed to do something different. It was not to be someone famous or influential, just different. It may seem humorous, but I never feel at ease or relaxed. I was constantly looking for what I was supposed to become. It was not obvious. There was no subject in which I performed better than others. I loved learning and reading about everything. When I tried to master something like an instrument or game, I would surpass those around me and soon become bored. I was often so lost in a book that I frequently burned dinner—or stayed awake until sunrise to finish it.

I felt odd and out of place, and people said I seemed like the oldest child. Wondering if I had been adopted, I also noted that it did not seem like my parents treated me the same way as my siblings. They were in every way encouraging and loving. But I would see a hesitance or flash of a questioning expression crossed their faces when it came to me alone and not my siblings. I looked so much like my aunts, uncles, and cousins as I grew older that I gave up the adoption theory.

I tried as many new things as possible and read every book in my school library. This was a fact that the librarian brought to my attention. She asked if there were any books I had heard of that she could order. She gave me a catalog to look through, but with a city library card, I often went there after school with my sister. I did not want the librarian to waste school money buying books already available at the city library. A free offer in a small corner of the catalog caught my attention. It was for a packet of brochures on hundreds of different occupations. When I showed her and asked if it could be ordered, she was delighted that I had caught something she had missed. She ordered two free sets.

In the meantime, it was still unclear what my profession should be. *Shouldn't God have shown me if He had any preference?* With no particular talent, I was at the top of my class in all the subjects taken in the college preparatory track. Maybe if I traveled, I would find the answer.

My dad had not finished high school when he journeyed from Georgia to New York to stay with his sister in search of a job. His mother had been well-known for her tasty cooking and made an income from running a small café at the front of their house. When he came to New York, he tried his hand at something familiar and succeeded. He went on to become a talented chef. It was one of his jobs when he met a friend of his sister's, my mom, and soon married her.

When they moved to Connecticut, he became a chef in a high-end department store. Always looking for opportunities to advance his career, they moved to California. He became a chef at an internationally famous luxury hotel. We loved his stories about all the famous people he cooked for, including US presidents. Although his heart led him to become a minister in our church, he resisted because of the income he needed from being a chef to raise his family of five children. He saw his only option was to focus on being the best at his cooking profession. In the evenings, he discussed this with friends and church elders while we played outside with their children. These discussions led to life-changing choices. Our family's journey changed gradually.

With my mom's support and encouragement, my dad completed the requirements to enter Bible school. They attended together in the evenings after very tiring workdays. My siblings and I played in the spacious DeSoto car's rear passenger area. My parents would park the car next to the city park in front of the school. It was dark and sometimes scary, but we brought our toys and were usually well-behaved. From the mixture of joy and concern on their faces after classes, they struggled with choices as my dad took on more responsibility at church.

It was not long after this that my dad developed a mysterious illness. His symptoms worsened at work. After tests and evaluations, it was revealed that he had become allergic to the main ingredients he used for his famous dishes and pastries. He was left with only one option, and the decision was made. His retirement from being a chef meant he could accept the assignment as a small rural church pastor. His embrace of this path was broader than he had expected. He became a community leader, shepherd, social worker, spiritual counselor, and spokesperson.

The little canyon we lived in had one entrance from the main two-lane highway. There was a way out that meandered through vegetable fields to an old road that ran briefly beside another busy freeway. This freeway was the only direct way over the mountains to Northern California. As my dad would say, we welcome all visitors who arrive at our home. They must have intended to come because no road allowed them to pass by on the way to somewhere else.

We would drive from the San Fernando Valley for an hour to get to the church where my dad was pastor. There were retired people among the permanent canyon residents. The best houses were those commissioned by affluent professionals from Los Angeles as summer homes or getaways. Our church was at the bottom of a hill, topped by a home owned by a dentist. Considering the convenience, size, and large yard, it was the perfect place for us to live. In addition, it was fully furnished with amenities we had only seen on TV.

I don't think we children ever knew the details. This was a problem of my family being poor, and the house's price was far more than we could pay. We just prayed that the dentist would be merciful and say yes to the money we had to offer. To my ten-year-old mind, it seemed my parents prayed, and God made the owner give us the house. We moved into a gadget-packed dream house with space to play. There were giant oaks to climb, surrounded by grassy hills to roam.

Our house was the site for many of our extended family holiday dinners and some of my fondest memories. My dad's cooking was always so good. Everyone had second and third servings. There was still room for some of Mom's sweet potato custard pie. My mom was the world's best yeast roll and sweet potato pie maker. Wafting through every room was laughter. Aunts gathered in the kitchen washing the dishes, with my dad's stories drifting in from the living room.

All of us had household and yard chores to do. My mom went to work during the day as a skilled and seasoned laboratory technologist. She also supervised the pathology department of a valley hospital. My dad was constantly called upon to put out some social fire or right a wrong.

As their children, we were supposed to perform well in school and stay out of trouble. After school and on weekends, we cleaned the church, pulled weeds in the flower beds, taught Sunday school, and sang as a backup choir if no other musicians showed up. Of course, we whined that we instantly became "volunteers" when no one else showed up to do a job.

In my mind's rearview mirror, I see how God molded us into servants who always rise to the situation. Sixty years later, we still excel at offering hospitality and unheralded service to others. It's second nature now, an automatic response whenever we encounter someone or a situation in need.

As an adult, years later, I often wondered how my dad felt about the sharp turn his life has taken in terms of profession, location, and duties. I never asked him because he died before the questions formed in my mind. But he mentioned clues as he discussed issues with his friends. Once, I heard him say that being a chef arouxnd famous people had been exciting. Advising powerful politicians on community issues had been a humbling opportunity for him, a poor boy from a small settlement in rural Georgia. But the deep satisfaction from serving spiritual meals to God's children had never been equaled. Despite everything, God had revealed a vision for his life. He was satisfied with what he was being allowed to do.

Maybe it doesn't matter where you start your journey. It is where you end up that counts. The problem is not knowing where to aim. I was good at studying and getting good grades, but that was not a profession. You must have money to go to college, and we didn't have any.

When my sister, two years older than me, was given a scholarship to a Christian university, other possibilities seemed available, even if we didn't have money. The problem was that there was still no answer to the question of what career to pursue.

In my junior year of high school, I was expected to be class valedictorian. Only three females earned the athletic jacket during our first year. There were no challenges I did not overcome. Maybe the challenges were too easy. I needed to get out and see if there was a challenge that would not be so easy to face. Unable to choose a profession, I decided not to attend college. Instead, I would travel around the world.

When my mom heard this, she stared at me as if I was speaking in a foreign language she did not understand. In hindsight, I cringe every time I remember this conversation. It must have frightened her deeply, but appearing undisturbed, she asked, "What prompted this decision?"

"Mom, I am bored to death with school. I want to explore and learn about the world differently," I explained, as only an arrogant, know-it-all teenager could, "This is not a foolish choice. I have been a straight-A student for five years, except for a B in geometry. I need something bigger than school to help me see what I should do with the rest of my life."

"How are you going to pay for this traveling?"

"In Europe, many young people hitchhike, live in hostels, and find jobs."

She continued to stare at me, then cleared her throat and stated she would make an appointment for me to see the doctor. Working in the hospital laboratory, she knew most of them. We never discussed why she chose to take me to see a doctor. I went, knowing I could defend my choice as logical. One doctor visit was not going to make me back down.

My doctor was very energetic, kind, and straightforward — everything I could hope for in a doctor. She started by asking questions, and the first two were intriguing.

"Do you know why your mom made this appointment?"

"Yes, she doesn't understand why I don't want to attend college."

"Yes, exactly. She says you are very bright and have never given her a problem. Why don't you want to go to college? Are you pregnant?"

"No. I want to leave that small canyon and see the rest of the world."

"You will need money if you want the power to decide where and when you will go from one place to another. Why not become a doctor? You can help people while you travel."

"First of all, I'm from a low-income family. We don't have money for medical school. Then, I'm Black. My sister and I often walk from school to the library to wait for our mother. This truck full of guys with a Confederate flag will drive by. They will yell at us to go back to Africa. I've never been and would not know how to get there. But I want to go and see it. What if it turns out that I do want to live there? And then there's the issue of being a woman."

"Yes, you have good points. Look. I can't change the fact that you are Black or a woman. However, more women are going to medical school these days. Some of us survived, even during my dinosaur days at medical school," she chuckled. "Seriously, if you return with an acceptance letter to medical school in four years, my group of women will pay for your medical school."

"You what? Are you kidding?" I had not expected this, and it would change everything.

"No, I'm not kidding," she said, shaking her head. She stared at me, waiting.

"Okay. I'll see you in four years. Get your money ready," I challenged.

"The money is already there. You're the one that has to get ready," she laughed.

I had things to do, like research schools, to apply to. I jumped up from my exam table seat and almost forgot to thank her as I left. I signaled to my mom that we could leave, and we walked from the lobby. I told her everything was fine when she asked how it had gone. But we needed to hurry up and prepare my financial aid and college applications, none of which I had bothered with thus far. She didn't ask questions but stifled the smile pulling at her lips. We were both in good moods, with a focus and direction. I was cured.

Fortunately, we managed to pull things together in time. After testing, I was awarded a state educational grant and other scholarships.

I was sure that after a quick run through undergraduate studies, I'd be heading to medical school.

Chapter 13

California - The World – Kenya

The relapse came three years later. I was beside myself with joy when I received an acceptance notice for a university senior abroad program at French-speaking universities in Grenoble, France, and Tunis, Tunisia. I had completed the premed requirements except for one class and was ready to leave for Grenoble in the summer.

Two months before my scheduled departure, my dad was in a severe car accident on his way to a county planning meeting. It was a single-car crash with a rollover in the freeway's grassy wide center divider. Had it been anywhere else along that roadway, it would have been instant death. When I saw him for the first time after the crash, he was in the intensive care unit at the hospital where my mom worked. I was shaken to see my strong dad look so weak. Never having seen or imagined him like this, I nearly fainted talking to him at his bedside. I struggled to leave the room to get a deep breath as the room grew dim around me. This experience affected me so profoundly that it changed my mind completely about pursuing a career in medicine.

Once, in the coolness of the hallway, I told my sister, "I just decided not to attend medical school. A real doctor would not faint in a patient's room. It's the wrong field for me. Fortunately, I've realized in time that I cannot possibly make medicine my career."

"But you've planned this for years. Don't make a decision based on one incident. I'm not saying you should change your mind. Take some time to let it simmer," said the future lawyer.

Tears stung my eyes, and arguing would only have worsened things. "Okay," I agreed.

My dad seemed to be getting better, but after several days in the intensive care unit, he died unexpectedly. Refusing to believe it was true, I was soon enmeshed in numbing grief as my life changed. I waded through my final exams and papers, desperate to escape into a new world. I did not allow myself to think beyond the surface. I had already become quite selfish and was determined to leave as scheduled. Three months later, I left for France and North Africa. I planned to return for graduation in one year, hoping things would be different after a year abroad.

***

A journey covering most of Europe, Scandinavia, North Africa, and several Sub-Saharan African countries ensued. This included visiting East Berlin and spending three days in a convent in Poland's city of the Black Madonna, exploring Egypt's pyramids, and spending seven days on a riverboat up the Nile and the Suez Canal. Unknowingly, four of us survived a deadly dust storm while sleeping under cars chained to a flat train car hurtling through the Sahara Desert and being captured by armed soldiers in Uganda. In the process, I almost died seven times.

I saw firsthand the severe shortage of medical professionals worldwide, leading to unnecessary death, disease, and suffering. Each scene left a lasting impression on me, making me stronger and more determined to recommit to the medical profession. I didn't know how, but I was convinced that I could find a way to get over fainting and make a difference in the world. I investigated options to attend medical school in France or Switzerland.

The world did change in many ways that year. Weeks before my planned arrival in Lebanon to pick up money and return tickets to the US, we were traveling from Kenya through Ethiopia. War broke out in Lebanon, blocking my way home and causing me to miss my graduation ceremony and other important deadlines. However, another unanticipated detour lay in store for me in the form of a challenge.

During this time, I received an invitation to teach in Kenya for two years. The offer was presented as an opportunity to help qualify students who would, in turn, attend medical school and provide healthcare in their country. My life changed in answer to this call. It was already too late to complete the one remaining class and apply for medical school when I returned. Deciding to return to teach in Kenya meant not being in the US to take the qualifying test the next year. I decided to wait and finish my commitment to teach for two years. I married, and we returned to teach in a rural area.

It was such a rewarding and successful experience that I began to view my medical school plans as unimportant and selfish. I decided

I would live there and raise our children. Unfortunately, after seven years, my marriage started a slow, agonizing march to its end as my American husband took a second wife. In Kenya, a man is allowed to have five legal wives, and thinking we would be in Kenya forever, he decided he could do as the Kenyans did. The truth was that the Christian church there only recognized one wife, but he explained this away. The non-Christian community had a rule that no man could take a second wife if it reduced the lifestyle of the first wife. It was another rule he did not feel obligated to follow.

This was the most significant, unwelcome challenge of my life. I didn't know what to do. I didn't understand how someone could do what they knew was wrong and believe they were the exception to even God's rule. He declared that the other people involved would have to get over their convictions or ignorant beliefs because he would be satisfied at everyone else's expense. Perhaps he would have had grounds for his decisions if he had succeeded, but he did not.

He was deluded and could not see that he was wandering down a road to destruction. I had a frightening dream that showed him in frail health unless he repented and chose to do the right thing. When I told him about my dream, he ridiculed me and accused me of trying to manipulate him. It seemed to become his greatest goal to prove me wrong as he slipped closer to the reality of what the dream had shown.

Insisting he was right caused him to abandon his wife, children, friends, church family, and pastor. My husband was withdrawing my entire direct deposit teacher's salary from the bank.

He had lost his job in the big city and would take it all if I couldn't get to the bank before he did. I started making latch-hook items to sell for money to buy food. He later said that he thought the community would rally around me to ensure the kids and I had food. I prayed for him to wake up.

Many miracles unfolded during this devastating time. I became an artist, designing the animals and scenes for the latch-hook creations I made. I hired a young lady to make them during the day while I taught school so we would have more pieces to sell. Also, visitors would arrive with food for us when we had no more food left. You may think this a horrible situation to be in. However, it is the tradition in Kenya that when you visit someone in a rural area, you bring a basket full of items. This is so that the household will not be ashamed if they have nothing fit to offer you for tea. Visiting people would bring sugar, bread, butter, cookies, and fruits such as bananas and oranges. So, visitors were always welcomed. In our case, the basket's contents would last many days, helping us get through until I could collect payment for the crafts I sold. I did not sleep nights, trying to make more things to sell. It was hard to sleep. I felt so lost, and he was not waking up.

What was I doing here? It was ridiculous. I was working hard day and night but had no way of assuring I could buy enough food for my children. I longed to find a way to improve the health of the communities around me, but I now began to doubt whether I could ever attend medical school. Could I ever be a more significant healthcare provider in Africa or elsewhere? My objective in coming to Kenya was to help citizens secure better healthcare by helping a larger number of students prepare for medical training. I wanted to do more. I received a giant positive nudge from an unexpected person.

My house was located at the farthest end of the school compound, enclosed with a barbed wire fence. In the neighboring yard lived a little girl who would hurry through her family garden of corn stalks. She would call excitedly from the fence for me to come teach her English. One day, I saw that one of her eyes was red and draining pus. When I asked her what had happened, she said her mother had told her an evil fly had put some bad things in her eye. She said that they had no money to get medicine. That eye would die, but she was glad she had the other eye to use.

I gasped, horrified that the little girl could accept the loss of vision in one eye so calmly. Health and fatalism walk hand in hand in the world of millions of people. I felt helpless because I had no money either. A sudden idea came to mind. When preparing to go overseas, I'd collected a sampling of medications in case I might need them. These comprised an antibiotic ointment, a cortisone cream, oral antibiotics, and bandages. More importantly, they included a small bottle of antibiotic eye drops. Not having seen it in a long time, a search for the same would be required.

"Go ask your mom if I can give you some medicine for your eye," I ran into my house to look for the tiny bottle, and she ran to ask her mom. I prayed I would find it and that it would work. I discovered the small bottle in the farthest, darkest corner of a dusty trunk. I was disheartened when I saw the expiration date had passed the year prior. "God help this to help her eye get better. It is the only thing I have."

The little girl called from the fence, "My mother says yes, teacher."

I walked out and, tilting her head back, placed the drops in her red eye. The little girl smiled, blinking. "Is that magic water?" she asked, studying the bottle.

"No. It's medicine, and you must come again for more before you sleep."

She returned for the drops over the next three days, and the pus disappeared while the redness reduced. Seeing the results filled me with such a sense of power and joy. Her eye would live to see another day. Passing her the bottle, I told her to have her mother do the same for the remaining days. She ran, holding the bottle aloft, like the Statue of Liberty's torch, and yelled joyfully, "I have the magic water."

Watching her figure disappear, I said, "Thank You, God, for saving her eye," and wondered aloud, "If I did that with no skills, imagine what I could do if I had training. I need to go to medical school. That's all there is to it."

***

My situation became increasingly unbearable, and I cried until there were no tears left in me. I began to think I was dying of cancer because of my rapid weight loss. Uncertainty and sorrow had caused me to lose eighty pounds, almost half of my weight. One thing was sure in my mind: I refused to die, leaving my children to suffer a life in a deluded, loveless, and unspiritual environment. I was determined to get them home and protect them from mistreatment.

Hearing God's voice was unequaled in its comfort factor during this horrible time. My continued stay in Kenya did not help anyone, so I asked my mom to send tickets for the kids and me to return to California. They were to be sent to the school address where I worked, not the regular PO box. I was so afraid of the intense emotional pain resulting from any interaction of any kind with their father. If any sign of my intended departure fell into the hands of their father, I imagined the resulting colossal fight and possible violence would be tragic. Emotionally exhausted, avoiding any more physical fights or arguments was a priority.

I was careful not to make any sign or mention of my plans. Their father had never visited our house at the new school. I secretly made a trip to Nairobi to apply for a passport for my baby. I was happy I was armed with the new passport and a few sweets for the kids. Of course, it was the one day he chose to visit. Upon my return, the neighbors and babysitter told me he had come by and said he would return later. My happiness deflated as I wondered what he wanted.

When he appeared in the evening, I was ready to explain my trip to Nairobi. It was to a salon to sell my makeup and hair curlers because there was not enough money to pay for our needs from selling the craft items. My heart skipped a beat when he asked if I had managed to get any money. I reported that it would be enough to meet our needs if I got paid for sales of the latch hook items to the craft shops at the Equator tourist site. My anger skyrocketed at the thought that he wanted to take more, despite already having taken my entire salary. I asked if he wanted to know because he planned to give us some of my salary. He backed down, promising to bring something the next time.

Because of his idea to bring items across the border, I had planned to leave while he was away. He came unexpectantly, the night of his departure, to leave the mistress's son in my care. My helper refused to stay with the child if I left. So, I was ready to cancel my trip rather than leave the baby in the hands of the people in town. I had heard rumors that many were angry at him for the many times he had wronged them. My heart sank as my plan to leave the country while he was away evaporated. It confused me as to why God would let something so unfair happen.

I prayed for understanding and resolved to let God do as He saw fit. A knock at the door startled me. My muffled weeping had overridden the sound of the returning car. They had come back with the idea that they could use the baby as a cover, saying they were visiting to show the baby to relatives. Never feeling so relieved, I thanked God for another answer to prayer.

Two days later, before dawn, we began our journey to the airport for the afternoon flight. Nervous anxiety occupied my mind all the way to the airport and persisted as we waited at the gate. After boarding the plane, my repeated glances out the window were in search of any sign their father had run onto the tarmac to drag us off and create an international headline-worthy scene. My eyes were shut tight as the speed increased heading down the runway. It was only when that feeling of weightlessness let me know we had left the ground. A deep, audible exhale escaped my lips when we were airborne. I was finally free of the prison of fear.

The flight attendants were incredibly kind on every flight, entertaining the children so I could sleep for a while. They seemed to know I was exhausted on every level. Although broken in spirit and heart, and with only a quarter in my pocket, I was at peace when I arrived at the airport twenty minutes from my mom's home.

My mom started crying when she saw us. "You look like war refugees," she said, taking the baby so I could identify our few pieces of luggage. Looking around, I noticed we were very thin compared to our fellow Americans. My considerable personal weight loss, I believed, was because I was dying from cancer. Not wanting to discuss this, I tried playing it down by saying it was because of increased walking and farming and reduced meat as it was too expensive.

She stared at me, shaking her head, and said, "Let's get you something to eat."

As I followed her out of baggage claim, peace settled over me. I felt hopeless about my future but so happy to have my children home in a safe place. It did not matter what happened to me after that. God had answered my prayer. My next goal was to work with the time I had left to live and pay my mom back.

Chapter 14

The Democratic Republic of the Congo

Two months after I moved to Kinshasa to get my Tropical Disease Certificate, rumors began circulating about power splinters among the church officials. I refrained from comment. I was not a church official nor privy to information that would give me solid ground to make any comment. More than this was my belief that God does not take sides in human battles. I knew the stories of Balaam and Joshua in the Bible when they met angels engaged in war in the spiritual domain. What is apparent to us in our struggles on earth is not the entire picture. I prayed that God would keep me on His side.

My extended stay at the church center lodging in Kinshasa was seen as evidence of my support for one side. I started looking for a house to rent and soon moved. The people who, as a united front under the leadership of the church head, had invited me to the DRC were no longer united. My efforts to have them meet and work out their differences were rejected.

***

When I visited the church clinic in Nkamba to bring pharmacy supplies, I saw that the head nurse had installed himself in the office I had occupied. He refused to give me the pharmacy keys to place the medication I had brought. He said the boxes of medication could be stored in his office for the present. To me, this indicated that he did not want an accurate count of what was being left.

His confident manner and disdainful attitude could only have come from his security in a belief that he had the backing of the church head. I knew I had been relieved of my director's duty without official notice. I had a revelation that this meant the application for the clinic to be designated as a hospital and receive government support and benefits would continue. It would be under my name but without my presence or input. I was angry and felt betrayed again.

Leaving the medication, I sent a message requesting an audience with the church head. The reply came that he was busy and would not see me until the following day. I could stay overnight at my house in Kindolo and speak with him in the morning. This was disappointing, but it sounded logical. My driver had been on the road since dawn and was tired. Some items left in my Nkamba house would be useful at my Kinshasa home. I could take advantage of the time to pack these, rest, and meet with the church head before returning to Kinshasa the next day. My steps became heavy, and I left the clinic to go to my car with a growing sense of unease and several questions.

As the car door closed, I immediately experienced a strong urge to return to Kinshasa. I looked out the window and over my shoulder to see if there was someone causing the feeling of a lurking menace. There was nothing in sight. The driver asked me what was wrong. Expecting resistance, I was hesitant but told him my feelings and desire to leave. He nodded in agreement, saying he felt the same menace spiritually, and we left immediately.

Days later, we heard that the head nurse had developed a plot to get rid of the staff I had hired and trained to manage the work—the vegetable garden project and the clinic accounts—successfully. They knew the strategy and process. The head nurse had not spent the time to understand the system in place for the village youth garden account funds or the hospital accounts.

After observing my other activities, he said he could easily replicate such simple things. These lies and claims had given him his job back. Unfortunately, he could not maintain the pharmacy stock, the garden, or the level of healthcare.

I was told the head nurse had reported that all of the medication I had delivered was expired, and he would make sure it was reported to the government in Kinshasa and destroyed. I don't know what happened after that, but the government never contacted me.

***

Reports of violence between church members surfaced. This jarred all of us. The church founder had commanded his followers not to take up weapons when the government came to arrest him. Since then, the church has always condemned and avoided violence of any kind. I called the church headquarters to find out if they were aware of these attacks and left a message asking the church head to send me an answer. I don't know if he received my message, but I never got a response.

The church officially split with a public declaration, followed by an order prohibiting meetings outside the one at single church center in Kinshasa. Anyone associated with specifically named church officials would be excommunicated. I had accepted a kind offer of lodging at the home of one of those named church officials.

Violent attacks were reported against those church members who were not willing to accept the split on political grounds, as well as the directive to refrain from associating with other church members. These spiritually wounded people gathered for prayer in the courtyard of the house where I lodged. Disappointed, fearful, and confused people gathered, especially on Sundays. To uplift the ousted members, officials allowed prayer services. Soon after, formal services were allowed to be conducted, bringing them great joy. Even greater crowds came to join them. I attended the group church in the house courtyard and was invited to be the main speaker at some church services. Many had stayed at home after the declaration of the split and mass excommunication. They hoped that the situation would resolve and everyone would reunite. I also prayed for unity and continued my Tropical Disease Certificate courses to prepare for what lay ahead.

***

Hearing that the church head would be in Kinshasa, I went to speak with him directly to understand what was happening and what he expected of me. I was given a chance to talk to him briefly. Another meeting of the two sides was set up but produced no reconciliation.

At my next meeting with the church head, I understood the two sides would not reconcile soon. After that day, no one from the Nkamba-based church answered my calls or messages. It was sad to realize that despite not changing, I was found unacceptable to a part of the church. I grieved losing the post I thought I was called to the DRC to fill.

It was now unclear what I was supposed to do, and I thought of returning home to the US. Maybe coming to the DRC was a big mistake, and I had misunderstood. But I had heard the "Now" command. It had been spoken so clearly that there could be no doubt. No one else had known about my dream. I had no idea where I was in my journey. I could have jumped from Nkamba. It was clearly behind me. Had Kinshasa been the new mountaintop, or was I still in the air? No "next" had been spoken. If it had, I had not heard it. I could still be in the air, jumping to the next mountaintop. The only thing I was sure of was that I was unsure about the future.

Chapter 15

"I hate this," I repeated for the hundredth time that morning, trudging along the road toward the taxi stand. On arrival, a conductor hanging out the open sliding door of a beat-up van called out my destination, and I dashed toward it. Clutching my small purse tightly, I navigated through the area known for pickpockets. My budget could not afford me to drop my purse or have any money stolen. There was just enough money to pay for the round-trip ride to the university hospital and buy a soda and a piece of bread for lunch. I pushed through the bustling travelers, hawkers, and circulating cars into the van door and past the conductor to claim a seat.

The ride was slow, with frequent stops to drop off or pick up passengers as we drove up the hill. Because I walked hurriedly from home each morning to the taxi stand, sitting on the crowded wooden unanchored bench inside the van gave me a chance to cool down and catch my breath. Rocking with the van's movement gave me a snapshot of everyday life as office workers, students, and professors hurried to their offices. Women taking their wares to market or bread from bakeries to shops for resale entered and left with large sacks of their goods carried on the roof rack. I learned some of the local language in the taxis. It consisted of commands spoken by the conductors and drivers without civility, courtesy, or good grammar. Having a big weight loss again, a question often came to my mind. What was going on, and why was I in this situation?

***

Through my university colleagues, I met members of the international medical community, a mixture of ex-patriots and representatives of private and foreign government aid companies. I was invited to give my opinions and input at many meetings. This did not lead to a job, but my friend later told me that many of my ideas were used in the organizations' funding proposals. He said I should apply for a job with them for planning or writing proposals.

He questioned, "Why would you continue giving valuable solutions away for free while you have no money to live on?"

An immediate answer came from somewhere deep inside me. "I am in the DRC to help. I was born without any ideas. Many people took the time to educate and support me until I could have these ideas. They are not mine. They have been collected from everyone I've met."

"Those are nice words. But have you ever thought of things from another perspective? Someone paid those people to educate and support you. Everyone should be paid for their part. It's how the world works. You are messing things up when you do it for free."

"I think that God will pay me somehow. If not, it's a sign for me to go home," I said.

Hope ebbed away, and I expected to be returning to the States soon. Missionary support donations from my home church made the move into a house possible. My food, housing, transportation, and utilities totaled around two hundred dollars per month. If you supplied material, a dress would cost ten dollars for a tailor-made outfit. All my clothes from the States were threadbare, and many were too warm to be suitable for the tropics. Fortunately, people often gave me beautiful fabric gifts, from which I would help design my tailor-made outfits.

On my few returns to the States, I found fabric outlet stores that sold remnant fabric pieces in lovely colors and designs at meager prices. You can imagine my surprise when I realized that my money-saving outfits had transformed me into a sort of fashion plate. The goal of being the best, most unusually dressed in the country was a real competition, which was not on my radar. People brought materials from other countries to turn them into tailor-made outfits. In many instances, the inexpensive materials I had purchased to make decent-looking outfits for myself had increased value because they were unique and unavailable for purchase by anyone else. I got compliments on them and questions from many about their source. It slowly became clear to me what was happening, and the pieces all fell into a clear mosaic in a very unusual way.

Running water was sometimes unavailable in our house for days. We kept our ears perked to hear air erupting in the pipes, signaling the water would soon return. Even if it came in the middle of the night, I rushed to wash everything I had. One night, I stayed up very late washing one bathtub after another full of two-piece outfits by color group. This included individually tailored tops and their matching full-length wrap-around skirts. I hung them on the clothesline stretched across the backyard until the lines were fully occupied. I hung my underwear across an improvised clothesline in my bedroom. Finally, tired from my workout, I fell into a heavy sleep.

Running late the following day, I ran out to gather my laundry inside. Finding it was still wet, I decided to let things dry thoroughly and collect them in the afternoon on my return. When I arrived, the lines were empty. I thought my housemates had been kind enough to bring them in. When I thanked them for the same, their blank faces made me realize they had no idea what I was talking about. *My clothes had been stolen.*

I was devastated to think that someone would jump over the surrounding wall, gather armloads of my clothes, and escape in broad daylight without fear of being seen. They must have collaborated with my neighbors, or the neighbors themselves were the thieves. They had a direct view of my yard and knew my schedule. I went outside and looked up at the terrace. Usually, one of the family members would sit there and wave to me. Today, it was empty, with the doors shut.

There was nothing I could do. If I reported the thieves to the police, the neighbors could easily slip a bribe to the investigating officer. He would write a false report saying he had thoroughly searched their house and found no supporting evidence of a theft. In retaliation, they might cause further damage or theft. I could hire a security guard but would have to pay a salary and provide meals, transportation, and healthcare. I had no treasures to guard worth that cost.

There was no money to buy replacement pieces for my wardrobe. The single outfit left was on my body. A prayer of thanks rose heavenward that my underwear had been inside. Although that meant a lot, frustration and anger boiled over in me. Why would God let these people do this and get away with it? There would be little gain for them but a grave loss for me. Most women had at the most four outfits: one for everyday wear, one for working around the house, one for special occasions, and one for Sunday church. Was it selfish to grumble about my ten outfits being stolen? Where was my "Hallelujah anyhow attitude"? A check-in with my spirit reminded me that God always has a good reason for everything happening in our lives. *Would I look for it?*

My search started with opening my old suitcases to find something to wear. I was delighted to see two stacks of beautiful forgotten material. These were from a one-woman show I'd performed in Los Angeles a few years prior—a show about the life story of a fictitious Kenyan woman. The background used was a line of twelve flowing ten-foot lengths of materials. These had lain in a cardboard box in my mother's garage for years. When clearing out my junk, I had thought I would try to arrange a show to raise money for the orphanage in the DRC. With all the activity around me, I had not considered it in a long time and had forgotten the material.

I started whooping and jumping around. Lying before me was a fantastic wardrobe, surpassing anything in the past. How great is our God? We may think we are doing something for one reason, but God knows the future and uses it to prove His love. It was something small on the world's scale, but it weighed tons on the scale of His concern for my wants and needs.

While I had little money, people must have thought I had come into a cash windfall. The tailor gave me a discount if she could keep the leftover material. Knowing I had not been to the States recently, some asked where the fabric for my new outfit had been purchased. Explaining how God had stored it for when thieves would steal all my clothes was an opportunity for many rejoicing sessions about God's goodness.

***

Months later, my financial situation improved significantly, and I bought a car. We were driving along the main street at the end of the work day. The street traffic was backed up, and bus stops were crowded. At one bus stop, something caught my eye in the crowd. A young woman waiting in line wore what looked like one of my previous outfits. I was so shocked that I told the driver to slow the car so I could get a better look at her. She stood with a crowd waiting behind her, looking like my neighbor's eldest daughter. Although she was probably unable to see me, my car was distinct because of its age and unusual color. I saw her head jerk toward my car, and she turned quickly, pushing her way into the crowd behind her.

She was gone when we made a U-turn and drove past the bus stop again. I couldn't confirm the truth of my suspicions beyond a shadow of a doubt. But my neighbors and all who had heard the story were eyewitnesses to God's bounty. It was clear proof of His provision for His children. He had displayed this evidence in the face of those who thought they could steal enough to discourage me or surpass His blessings.

*****

My high "Certificate with Distinction" mark at the end of my six-month studies surprised everyone, including me. My verbal French skills and vocabulary were not at the level required for everyday conversation. My exams in each department were formulated to test my practical observation of symptoms and identification of diseases from tissue or blood slides and disease vectors. It was new and exciting material, and I studied hard. As a result, my French medical vocabulary blossomed.

Unfortunately, my knowledge of Lingala was still rudimentary. This was fine for everyone but me. Everyone around me wanted to learn and practice speaking English. As a result, I was learning very little of the local language. My inability to speak the local language meant I couldn't see patients independently in a regular clinic. How would I find a job helping people in the DRC?

Fortunately, God strengthened my trust in His ability to provide unexpectedly. Before I received my first check for clinic work for the US government, my pockets were empty. The extra cost of gas to drive to work was more than I had anticipated. So, borrowing ten dollars from a friend at church, I headed home reassured of the fuel needed until payday. On my way home, a young man I knew from church flagged me down and asked me to drop him off near my destination.

In the morning, I checked my purse to transfer the ten-dollar bill to an easy-to-access holder in my car. It was nowhere to be found. I turned my purse inside out and checked the car's floor and under the seats. Nothing. I checked the ground around the car and the yard, then went inside and retraced my steps to the bathroom and bedroom. Nothing. As a last resort, I called my housemate and asked her to help me search through everything again. We found nothing.

Time was slipping away, so I decided to risk and coast most of the way downhill into town. There would be a chance to borrow the money or get an advance before heading home. What other option was there? Asking my housemate to open the gate so I could drive out of the yard, I gathered my things. She ran barefoot to get her shoes.

Hearing yelling and stomping in the hall, I ran out to see what was happening. She was terrified, pointing at the floor, stomping, and yelling, "Nyoka! Nyoka!" (Nyoka means snake.)

I looked at the floor, and a five-foot-long snake was slithering toward her.

Grabbing her arm to get her attention, I said, "Go get the garden hoe. We have to kill it.

She looked at me, confused, as if I were crazy. This was probably because the hoe was in the hall closet beyond the snake, and she had not thought to go out the side door and around. The snake stopped suddenly and vomited a dead rat covered with slime. It then turned and slithered into the partially open door beside it. She went into a complete frenzy, screaming with widened eyes, making it impossible for me to think of options. The snake had entered her bedroom.

I had an idea to get her out of the way and bring help. I yelled over her shrieks that she should run down the block and get the owner of our rented house. "Tell him he needs to come with a machete and kill the snake. Hurry," I urged her.

Her glazed eyes focused, and she calmed. "Yes, I will go get the owner," she said. In total abandon she ran down the hall behind me and out the side door in her bare feet.

Somehow, I expected that the owner would not be at home. It was up to me to kill the snake before my housemate returned. I ran to get the hoe, returned to the ajar bedroom door, slowly opened it, and switched the light on. There were clothes, shoes, and papers piled against the surrounding walls. The snake could be hiding anywhere. How was I supposed to find it in time?

"Lord," I prayed. "Show me where the snake is." A bright white arrow appeared on the wall a few feet from the door, like a blinking neon sign, pointing to a spot of stacked shoes and purses. Holding the long hoe handle, I lifted shoes and bags one by one with the edge of the hoe blade. I felt displaced to a bright corner of the ceiling to my right with someone floating beside an ethereal me. While in conversation, we watched the earth-bound me removing items. At the bottom of the pile, the coiled snake was next to the plugged-in phone charger.

From the corner of the ceiling, I heard my earth-bound self say, "Sorry, Mister Snake, but I am late for work and have to kill you before my housemate returns." Closing my eyes, I struck with the hoe several times in rapid succession. When I opened my eyes, I was standing, gripping the handle, and looking at bloody pieces of snake on the floor. The ceiling corner was empty.

Panting from my efforts, I heard my housemate return. She breathlessly said the owner was not home, and I heard her open and then close my bedroom door.

Her voice was worried as she called, "Mama Joyce? Where are you?"

"I'm in your room."

"No, you must come out of there. The snake will kill you."

"I killed the snake. Come see."

"You what?" She entered the room and saw me pointing to the chopped-up snake.

"I killed the snake," I repeated, shuddering for the first time.

Her look of surprise changed to disappointment. "Oh, look, you destroyed my charger." She took a closer look and grabbed the hoe handle from my hand. "You didn't crush the head. It can still bite you." As if on cue, its mouth repeatedly opened and closed in spasm.

Crushing the snake's head with the blade until it was deadly still, she said, "There, he is done."

She returned the hoe handle to my hand and refused to take the pieces to the garbage burning pit in the front yard. I relented to do so. Otherwise, I would arrive even later at work.

When I arrived late for work but without stopping or stalling, I gave my exciting excuse. My colleagues looked up the snake based on my description. They were anxious because it was poisonous. One loaned me money for gas. They all cautioned me never to try to kill a snake, adding that I should *never* close my eyes to one coiled up before me. I started shaking after a while, thanking God.

When I returned home, my housemate explained why she had been so terrified in the morning. A few nights before, she'd had a dream of sleeping in her room after the rest of us left for work. A poisonous snake had come and bitten her, and she had died before anyone came home. Seeing the snake, she had imagined her nightmare coming true. When it entered her room, she had been sure she would die. After I left, she called one of the church officials to report the incident, and he said that God had prevented a great tragedy.

I had placed the money loan for gas in my purse, but that ten-dollar bill was never seen again. Miracles appeared on several levels in its place. Its loss had caused me to wake my housemate to help me search for it. She had seen the snake before it entered her room and hid. An extraordinary revelation of its hiding place leading to its ultimate death without harm to any one of us. God had arranged the timing for all of these activities. He showed an example of His power and love by answering our prayers to prevent hurt or harm. We continue to pray for His protection for ourselves and others from dangers, seen or unseen, known or unknown.

Chapter 16

You can imagine the depth of my discouragement, trying fruitlessly to find a job or source of income. I had reached my limit and was ready to go home. Sitting and praying fifteen minutes before the Sunday service started in the courtyard, I whispered to God, "It doesn't seem like a good witness for me to claim to be on a mission for you if there is a constant lack of provision. I don't know if it's the wrong path, timing, or place. So, I will put out a fleece, just like Gideon did in the Bible, and ask for a miraculous sign to show me the right choice. God, if You provide a source of income from your intervention, I will stay. If not, I will go home."

Right before the opening music started, my phone rang. It was the health provider at the American Embassy. He explained that he had a family emergency and he needed to leave for the States and asked if I could fill in for several weeks until the new permanent provider arrived. What an answer to prayer! It was more than the living wage I had hoped for. The resulting funds were used to buy more than food and transportation. Unexpected opportunities were presented to purchase land for the orphanage. Finally, something good and lasting was happening that others would see as an example. This would be my legacy for the DRC.

While the orphanage was being built, another big idea came. In alignment with my desire to improve local general health, a small team would train people in various communities to organize an HMO-type community-based limited healthcare insurance. In designated areas, people could pay a monthly fee to have access to care for the ten most common preventable and easily treatable illnesses. These included malaria, urinary tract infection, and diarrhea. A family member was required to attend the ten disease prevention classes before the family joined.

Supplies would be given to specific community clinics for members' disease diagnosis and treatment. No hospitalization or treatment of diseases outside of the ten would be covered. The program's success was based on a small, consistent payment for each person covered and the logical expectation that few would be sick simultaneously. This process went well. Many households were trained on diseases and prevention. The network grew, and community leaders who wanted fame and election surety joined the support advertising. The plan was for each area to organize and manage its program. Our training team would then move to arrange a new location.

We made great strides until some employees focused on personal gain instead of supporting the program. Lies and the failure of those who knew better to report dishonest acts destroyed the program's effectiveness and reputation. I was shocked. The initial staff had been selected based on experience and pastor character recommendations. They were earning good, regular salaries and a stable source of provision for their families. Despite leaving the tenuous arena of no salary to a regular income, some were dissatisfied that even more money did not flow into their hands.

Our membership enrollment, fees, and salary payment systems made embezzlement impossible. So, some stopped doing their jobs when they came or stopped coming regularly except for paydays. They threatened their fellow workers, so they did not tell us. We did unannounced quality checks and found out anyway. The culprits were fired, and the program was handed over to community leaders after a short training period. Letters of recommendation were given to the faithful employees, who went on to bigger and better jobs.

It was a painful experience, and it took me a while to climb out of that pit of despair. I wrestled with the heartbreak of seeing my fellow church members steal from their communities. I grieved for how the selfish choices of a few wrong people could thwart the benefit intended for many. God gives free choice. It is His affair with every person. My choice was never to support wrongdoings and let God sort out other people's hearts.

The rest of the money earned from the embassy was used to underwrite the orphanage program. I expected to be relieved from further service when the new healthcare provider arrived. However, at her request, a part-time position was created for me to see patients referred one day per week. Becoming familiar with the embassy staff was an excellent opportunity to display my skills and character. Because of this, another option opened up for me.

An American and his team contacted me to help establish and manage a new hospital's human resources department. This gradually grew into supervising the hospital's hiring of the initial staff and writing protocols, job descriptions, and policies for human resources activities.

It was a challenging opportunity to learn some essential lessons about applying international quality goals in the context of cultural norms and bias. Being helpful, doing a good job, and standing for quality and honesty made me happy. However, working without support from the people around me often made me feel quite sad and discouraged because, for many, their most potent driving forces were financial and power greed.

Determined as I was to do my best in God's eyes, my life was threatened through notes and rumors, false accusations, false witnesses, and acts of sabotage perpetrated against me. Despite my sacrifice of time and effort, allegations of wrongdoing were hurled against me. Perhaps it was culturally wrong to abruptly insist that things be done in order and by adhering to a quality standard. Neither the government, the society, nor the employees recognized a benefit in how I set things up. However, the remarkable results were applauded despite the debate on the process.

It was tiring to hear people insist without evidence that improvements could be achieved using systems and processes that had failed despite years of application. Colonial powers had established outdated systems before national independence. Since then, these have been updated and changed in the colonialist countries. So, why not change for evidence-based improvements? Establishing quality standards for all my full and part-time employees was a daily battle.

One day, exhausted after work at the embassy, I headed home for a nap instead of shopping. Home was the place I was house-sitting while the owner—a friend—took a vacation. My eyes had just closed for a nap on the living room sofa when my phone rang. My hospital boss was returning my earlier call. Discussing work, I was startled by an army tank-like sound passing by the house.

"Hold on a minute. I have to check something out," I told my boss.

All sleepiness left me as I hurried to the front window. Visible through the spirals of razor wire stretched along the top of the high-security brick wall was an incredible sight. With a frown on his face, the blue-helmeted head of a UN peacekeeping troop was gliding down the capital city's main street. I couldn't see the vehicle, but this made my heart race, and a chill shook me. Goosebumps rose on my arms and spread slowly. This could not be true. I jerked the curtain closed to shut out the image, and my legs barely carried me to sit on the sofa.

"What's going on? Are you there?" asked my concerned boss.

The hand with which I held the phone had dropped to my side. I replaced the phone to my ear. "Yes, I'm here. I don't know what's happening, but I need to hang up and call the embassy to find out." He insisted I explain what was causing me to be afraid. I quickly explained, hung up, and tried to contact the embassy. The call went unanswered.

Seconds later, there was a thud against the house's front wall. Then came the sound of glass breaking, and the front window where I had just stood shattered. A sharp puff of air pushed the curtain toward me. Broken window glass pieces fell to the floor, blocked by the drawn curtain. The other front window shattered as I ducked and crawled toward the safety room.

Panting, I sat on the safety room bed, wondering what was happening. My heart raced as bursts of gunfire sounded from all directions, surrounding the house and hitting other areas of the front walls. Continued attempts to call the embassy were to no avail. Maybe they were overwhelmed with calls from people like me, needing information or further instructions. I called my fellow worker and friend in the embassy clinic using her cell. She reported that everyone had been sent home just after I'd left and told to shelter in place. She had no idea what was happening but would notify security that shots were heard at an American's house on the main street.

Security called shortly afterward to say they had been unaware anyone was in the house since the employee had left the country. Had they known, an evacuation alarm would have been sent to me at the first sign of danger. The present situation involved rogue soldiers attacking a house in the next block. This placed me in the center of the fighting hotspot. The only intervention possible was instructions to stay quiet in the safety room without lights, radio, or loud conversations that might attract attention. They would alert me of any further news.

The prophetic story I had heard years prior came to mind. That man had said I must not forget there was no need to fear bullets when I was on a mission. How does one minister to a city during lockdown? Calling friends, I told them of my hope that the fighting would be limited and not spread anywhere else, and we prayed together. When it was too late at night to call anyone, I played solitaire and whispered songs of praise under my breath.

There had been no voices or movement inside the yard, even with the most vigorous shooting exchanges. The next day, hunger prodded me to take a risk. During a lull in the shooting, I opened the safety room door and ran barefoot to the pantry. I grabbed a sack full of granola bars, a jug of water, and a crate of sodas, then tip-toed back. I suddenly thought of the security guard who had faithfully been there to open the gate when I drove in or out. If he were still alive, he would need some food as well. I tip-toed back to the pantry to grab some of the same things. I edged the side door open a crack to peek out. The guard was crouching down in the far corner of the carport.

He signaled me to close the door. "It's not safe. Go back inside," he whispered.

"Are you okay? I asked.

"Yes, Madam. I am fine."

"Are you hungry?"

"Yes, I am very hungry," he whimpered as his shoulders dropped.

"Here," I said, placing handfuls of granola bars on the step.

"Thank you, Madam. God bless you." He gave a sign of gratitude. "Now go back to safety."

"Don't worry," I assured him. "Everything will be all right."

He nodded and motioned me to close the door. I heard the crinkling of granola bar packages through the slit at the door bottom. I hurried back to the safety room with the new supplies.

After three days, the silence persisted. My friend from the embassy clinic called. The shelter-in-place order had been lifted, and she would pick me up in ten minutes.

When she arrived, I stepped outside the house for the first time in three days. I had never known such silence at the center of town. Not even the birds were bold enough to resume their songs after such a persistent deluge of artillery. The security guard had opened the gate for her. His uniform was severely wrinkled, and his eyes were bloodshot and sleepy. But he was smiling and walked with quick steps, apparently uninjured. He clasped his arms across his chest in a motion of gratitude, then patted his stomach, smiling. I was happy to have thought of him.

The three of us inspected the damage done to the outside of the house. There were many gouges and holes made by bullets, big and small, on the exterior facing the street. None of the ammunition had pierced through to the interior other than the two shattered windows.

My car, parked on the street side next to the two shot-out front windows, stood with its windows intact. One flat front tire had an associated bullet hole in the surrounding mudguard. It would not have been possible to drive anywhere if I had wanted to. God had sent my friend to rescue me. What a true friend with a good heart and a blessing on multiple occasions.

A few bodies lay beside the road as she backed her car out of the yard. The streets were silent and otherwise empty as we moved toward her house. Not one living person was visible.

She created a safe haven in her home and welcomed me as part of the family. I was able to focus on my work without distractions. Life seemed to return to normal for a while, except for the tired women begging on busy corners and the groups of hollow-eyed, ragged street children who soon reappeared.

Chapter 17

There were problems in Kinshasa. Understanding them was impossible without having some knowledge of the city's history and unique context. It was explained to me by professionals, beggars, local and foreign, and from many sides after I had asked many questions over a long time. It was shocking to realize that in this African city, the cost of living was among the highest in the world. Plopped down in the middle of malnutrition and lack of plumbing, unpaved streets, and potholed roads were grocery stores with any product you could think of. It was not limited to some dark corners, duty-free shops for foreign military employees, or the black market. European and American brands were on the shelves of stores every day. If you had the money to pay for it, everything was available. I was amazed to find fresh cherries in the produce department one day. Cherries were my favorite fruit, and I could not resist paying the price of a full dinner for a handful imported from South Africa. They disappeared quickly after I washed them at home. With my eyes closed, I savored the taste of the happy memories of wandering through cherry orchards in California with my children. We had run laughing from tree to tree, stuffing our mouths with as many as we could pick to take home.

The DRC was enormous in terms of sheer land area, the second-largest country in Africa, and the eleventh-largest in the world. It was also the most populous Francophone country in the world. Politically, it was systematically united by language. That such a large country with multiple tribes had been united this way was a lesson for the world. There was constant war and frequent skirmishes for access to minerals along its eastern borders, shared with five countries. Kinshasa, where I lived, was over a thousand miles away, near the Atlantic Ocean, far from any war activity or social impact. Inside shops or restaurants, I heard a world full of different languages. People of various nationalities had a high demand for foreign products from their home countries, and they had the financial means to purchase them at imported prices.

Across many African countries, most people were poor, except for foreigners with an income from abroad, savvy or corrupt politicians, or the traditional ruling class. Many foreigners had lived in Kinshasa for years, working in long-established businesses, organizations, or embassies. There were clubs and sports activities that you could find in most European cities. Some families were three or four generations deep in the culture and spoke local languages.

But people were discussing how things were changing for the worse. Recently, foreigners from economically disadvantaged countries moved into every neighborhood in Kinshasa. They were not interested in putting down roots or having a luxurious lifestyle. One of them that I spoke to explained that they were driven by desperation and starvation at home. Their government had underwritten travel and start-up costs to establish a market for products from their country. If successful, they could support their families back home, thus saving them from death by starvation.

They aimed to develop a market for products imported from their home country. They would investigate what people wanted to buy and open a large shop with an attractive variety—not in a new area but right next to an establishment that had been there for years. I was told this was intentional because that was where people were accustomed to coming for the products. When people saw the same type of things sold at a lower price next door, they would buy it. They found later that the items were less durable. Once the local owner was forced to close, the foreigner with an established monopoly would raise prices at will, and the foreign country's economic hold would be strengthened on the nation as the money generated would be sent out of the country.

To some degree, this was happening at every level. My friend made a daily living selling fresh, warm beignets to neighbors passing her established spot on their way to work. The woman woke early in the morning to make beignet batter and carry the oil and cooking fire materials to her spot. Her friends did the same thing to earn money to buy food for their families. They began arriving at their regular place only to find a foreigner with a high-capacity deep fryer in full swing. Her friends and neighbors gladly bought from the new seller because they did not have to wait, and the price was slightly less. The women were devastated, unable to compete with the prices offered by the new competition, who bought all their ingredients at wholesale prices. They were forced to find locations to sell farther walking distances from their homes and with fewer clients. The economic platform for these women looking to be saved from begging was eroding.

My friends had heard some sad news from family members who had remained in rural areas. The land their families had used for subsistence farming and manual mining for diamonds or gold was being sold to foreigners. The political leaders got the money for this deal, and they promised to share it with the community to establish schools and clinics. It was soon squandered, legal agreements were violated, and foreign investors claimed default possession of the land. Fences were erected, and people found they were barred from using the land to raise food. The economic plight was worse than in town.

It was curious that the erstwhile cultural and social support also failed due to the economic environment. If a man died, leaving his widow and children living in the house on his family's land, she had two choices. After the mourning period, she could marry one of her dead husband's brothers or be thrown out of her home. The fact that she had helped build the house or worked the land to provide food for the family or to sell for income would not even be considered. With HIV rampant and the fickleness of these brothers in the treatment of their children, many women didn't like the option of marrying a brother-in-law. Also, as money was scarce, the brothers preferred to have one of their children move into a built and furnished house. They sent the woman back to her pre-marriage family or big cities. Many of these widows streamed into large cities, seeking work in the homes of wealthy or foreign households to earn food for their children. This job market was soon saturated. They were thus forced to become street beggars without a home. The older children, deprived of an education, turned to crime.

There were rumors of a collaboration with some policemen willing to look the other way in exchange for a payoff by the gangs. The government often did not pay the street police or paid them poorly, and they, in turn, resorted to graft and bribery. On many occasions, I was stopped for a trumped-up traffic violation and presented with an offer to accept a cash on-the-spot payment at a fraction of the fine required for a citation.

Many crimes became bolder and more violent. There was an increased number of street children swarming the city streets. Every day on my way home from the hospital, I thought someone should do something about this growing problem. The explosion of young children and women begging on the street corners was striking in the short period since I had first come to Kinshasa. My curiosity increased about the source of the streams feeding this growing sea of children without homes, food, or supervision. There were some aspects, such as the constant wars and attacks from neighboring countries in the east, that only the government could address. However, citizens could address certain other aspects with initial support from funds and training. These aspects offered possible high impact with an added facet of self-sustainability.

Many international organizations were investing in rounding up the street children and putting them in boarding schools in the area.

If the boys had been in street gangs, they rarely adjusted to being in disciplined environments. Despite having to face the cold, hunger, and violence, they returned to their familiar friends and lifestyle. An earlier intervention was needed.

Why not start a project where mothers were trained to earn a living, support their families, and stop the vicious cycle? I accompanied a church official to Washington, DC, to meet with funders, and our proposals were approved. We only needed confirmation from the local official.

On our return, one organization sent a representative to visit us for a first-hand investigation. We ferried them around the town to meet other agencies and gather the information needed to verify our proposal. We were shocked that they had instead agreed to partner with one of the agencies we had taken them to meet as an example of a poor approach.

In the office of another local director, I was told to enter his office very disrespectfully, where he was laughing and joking with a man asking for funding for his project. Made to explain our project in the presence of this other project proposer, I gave a summary and tried to hand the director a copy of the detailed project. He sneered and said he would not give me any of "his money." He refused a copy of the proposal and asked no questions about our research. He turned away from me to continue talking to the other man. My heart sank, and I walked out of his office, taking deep breaths to keep from crying. That had been my last funding hope.

I applied unsuccessfully for several other job positions, but my rejections each time seemed to be due to people's wrongful attitudes and assumptions about me. I believed that God did know me and was placing these hurdles and closing doors in my path for reasons to be clarified later. However, at the time, it felt like a deep, aching pain with no way of healing.

***

Despite no means of supporting the widows' training program, the staff was interviewed, and protocols were written. A steady flow of funds or a significant initial sum was needed until I found a new job to provide the money. I headed to the travel bureau to buy a ticket home.

Yards away from the travel agent's door, I heard my name called. An old friend rushed toward me. He had been looking for me to help him write a proposal that needed to be in English, and the pay would be generous. At last, the answer to my prayer for provision for the project and, hopefully, a herald of things to come.

As usual, I gained valuable lessons and insight into the workings of being a consultant for a UN organization from the perspective of working with governmental and fellow international organizations in the trenches. Anxious to finish it, receive my check, and see what lay down the road, I sat typing the last pages.

Without special prayer or me offering a spiritual fleece, my phone rang with a call from an out-of-the-country area code. The caller said he was calling from the World Health Organization (WHO) because my name had been highly recommended for consideration for a new project post. He asked if I was interested in being interviewed for a job that seemed to fit me like a glove. It was a tailor-made opportunity that would use my experience, cultural understanding, and language skills to draft a practical and adaptable program for use in different countries.

My first thought was that this was a scam. I was confused, not daring to hope this was a real offer from WHO. I said, "Thank you for the call. I don't believe you, so I am hanging up," and ended the call. *The nerve of some people,* I thought. Returning to completing my task, I was surprised when the same number called me again. Thank God, this man was very patient. After that conversation, I engaged in the application process, leading to one of my life's most incredible journeys. My post as the WHO program's African regional manager of a life-changing project lasted seven years and positioned me to consult on other projects. There were some surprises.

Geneva and the African Regional Headquarters decided I should move to Ethiopia for easy flight access to six countries the program initially catered to. How disappointing for me to be required to live outside of the DRC. We had just started our orphanage and widow training project, and there was no turning back. It was the chance of a lifetime to impact the health of African families. It would also supply money for the DRC's women's training and primary school projects.

The program manager's office was located in Geneva, Switzerland, in a building I had visited thirty years ago. My search for a job as a translator was unsuccessful, and I had no idea that my future would bring me back in a very different capacity. My boss had assembled a united and committed team with managers in the African and UK regions. The program was built on existing partnerships between UK and African hospitals. For years, the partnerships have addressed various health issues. Our program strengthened these partnerships through increased interactions, the introduction of protocols, sound evidence, internationally accepted methods, and printed materials. It brought powerful results and gained an audience for other healthcare programs in Africa.

My duties required onsite hospital investigation, research of the country's health system, medical support, and pharmaceutical distribution. Initially, the immense impact on national healthcare beyond the specific hospitals involved was unclear. I was encouraged one late afternoon when the finance officer in the Ministry of Health agreed to see me for a few minutes.

He hurried into the conference room and said, "You have been very persistent, but we are tired of your people coming here and trying to get us to spend a lot of money we do not have."

"Sir, I think you have the wrong idea. I am here to show you how to save money."

"What do you mean?" He frowned and sat down.

I said, "Give me the money you usually spend on cholera yearly. I will stop the annual epidemic and refund 90 percent to you."

He laughed in disbelief and said, "How will you be able to do this?"

"I will employ the 10 percent to train hospital staff on the protocols and procedures for diarrhea abatement. These have successfully been used to run a campaign to stop the expensive annual epidemic."

"Do you have any study papers about this?"

"Yes," I said, searching my briefcase. "I have a copy of several studies."

"Great. I will personally take these to the minister of health," he said, taking the papers in hand. He stood and smiled. "This has been quite unexpected and very welcome. Saving money was not what I was anticipating. Thank you." He left, shuffling through the papers given to him.

This was not the only unusual opportunity I experienced. There were two main factors we had not taken into consideration. The first factor was the critical mass of research results of antimicrobial studies in countries at the same economic level that allowed the development of practical cost-saving strategies. The timing created a golden period that opened the ears of the decision-makers to low-cost activities that could reduce their country's disease rates. Whereas people thought we were bringing expensive, other-worldly ideas that were not economically feasible, we presented practical, economical ideas of simple interventions and hope. We were hope-filled and convinced of the power of good evidence to ignite imaginations and realize dreams. The second was that the large hospitals in partnerships were usually the country's largest health institutions and training centers where newer practices were applied and closely watched. Sometimes, an idea in the right hands at a critical moment brings success. God is good at setting up critical moments and moving people to the right places.

***

The constant tropical weather in the DRC had made my winter clothes useless, so they remained in the States. However, the weather in mountainous Ethiopia was cold, especially in the mornings and evenings. In addition, there was snow on the ground at times in Geneva. During flights, I often changed from sandals to socks and shoes, wrapped skirts to pants, and a sweater, or vice versa. So, I had two separate wardrobes in my suitcases when flying to meetings.

Most women in sub-Saharan countries wear brightly colored cotton outfits year-round. I had adopted the same fashion. When I returned to the States on a break, the newest sets and gifts for friends and family were packed in a carry-on-sized bag in two empty, prominent cases. The plan was to fill them with supplies on my return. My warm clothes were in a suitcase or closet at my mother's house.

In the States, I shopped for simple items that would make a big difference at the DRC project compound. On my return flight, my suitcases were filled with these things and toys for the orphans. Passing through the long DRC immigration lines brought on the uneasy apprehension of facing customs agents at the airport's arrival gate. Having been profiled by the plane I came on and for my accent, there seemed to be agents looking for a chance to be paid off for not checking bags, going through bags and confiscating items, or charging import taxes in cash. The cash was slipped into their pockets openly. No receipts were ever given. No one was held accountable. It was a very frustrating experience. It did not matter to them that someone was trying to do something good and loving for orphans.

On arrival one sweltering afternoon, I was exhausted in the non-air-conditioned arrival area. Retrieving my bags from the conveyor belt, I prayed, "Dear Lord, please let me pass through as if invisible. What they are doing is wrong and hurting your little orphan." Then, taking a deep breath, I pushed the laden cart toward the exit door. None of the agents noticed me as they watched people walking toward them. One agent's head jerked up sharply, looking in the distance without a focal point as if he had heard something coming from my direction. The agent did not notice my passing and looked through me as if he could not see me. He held his hand up, halting the person following me. I exited the building without breaking my stride. This was a miracle.

Chapter 18

The initial process of getting approval for full-time work at WHO seemed endless. When I got the opportunity to work on a short project associated with an American organization in South Africa, I was glad to take it. Not long after this, I arrived from South Africa and hurried to be one of the first in line to get through immigration. The next open agent looked me over and slowly searched through my passport. This was not a good sign, and it was not surprising when he informed me that my visa was noncompliant with immigration regulations. During my time outside the country, the immigration rules for my type of visa changed. There was no way I could have known about the change. He did not accept this and continued shaking his head no matter what I said. When he said I would have to return to South Africa on the next flight, it convinced me he wanted a bribe. I stood by his booth as he processed other people, glancing at me frequently.

Having decided not to engage in the bribery system, I stood still, waiting to see his next move. God had not made it clear if he wanted me back in South Africa or not. Until there was clarity, there was no need to worry one way or the other. Meanwhile, the driver who had been sent to pick me up entered the immigration section through the baggage claim area to see what was happening. I told him what the agent had said.

He attempted to speak with the agent, who became enraged that he had entered the immigration area. The agent said I would return to South Africa on the next flight. He added that any further interference from the driver would be illegal, and he would be arrested if he did not leave the area. The driver assured me he would notify this agent's superiors and left.

The agent then insisted my presence disrupted the immigration process and led me to a room with just a chair and table. He demanded I sit there and talk to no one until my plane was ready to board. With a raised voice, he said that I must not understand how serious my situation was and then slammed the door. I felt he stood outside the door briefly, hoping he had frightened me, and was waiting for me to exit and offer him something. But no bribe was going to come. Still unsure if God wanted my return to South Africa, I prayed, quietly singing one of my recently written songs, and waited.

The agent returned a short time later and flung the door open. He asked angrily, "Are you singing? Do you know you are being sent out of this country?"

I replied, "You will do what you have to. But it's God who will decide."

He hissed, "You are impossible." He looked at my passport and then tossed it on the table. "Get out of here. Take your passport and go."

"Thank you," I said calmly. Walking through an empty immigration hall, I quickly found my baggage, the last pieces on the conveyor belt. As I walked out of the exit, no customs agents were present. Waiting outside, the driver was pacing with a worried frown as he talked on the phone. He lit up with a smile and ran over to grab my luggage and take me home. I didn't know all the phone calls and prayers that had gone up in the interim. God's response was deliverance.

***

One night, a piercing question broke through my sleep and set me bolt upright in bed. Was this why I had come to the DRC? This was the job God had allowed the network head in California to hear and describe in the papers he'd given me. If Papa had hinted at the details of this idea during my first visit, my probable reaction would have been that it was an impossibility in Africa. We can't imagine what lies around the bend in the road. Maybe it was not for one Nkamba hospital but for many hospitals. We go on an unexpected life ride as God reveals His will and plan.

The interlaced paths of the orphans' and widows' projects ran parallel to my healthcare activities. I used vacations and holidays to visit the in-progress construction of the DRC projects. The two above-ground floors were for an orphanage, and the basement classrooms were for the widows' training. We hoped that my mom would come to the dedication of the orphanage named after her, Evelyn's Arms. I was sad that she was becoming too weak for the long journey. We moved the dedication ahead to before the orphanage's completion. However, it soon became evident that my mother's failing health would not allow her to attend even on that date. My sister came to represent her and give her blessing.

While touring the structure, the architect asked me which color to choose for the paint of the exterior. Everyone thought I'd go with a shade of blue, my favorite color. But standing before the building, I saw it shimmering in yellow, and my mind flew back over decades.

After my Sunday school experience to commit my life to God, when I was nine, I began having a recurring dream. In it, there was a big yellow house full of children speaking a foreign language. They wore school uniforms and ran around playfully, laughing and tugging on one another. I stood in the hallway, admonishing them to be serious. "You are here because you are called to do something special. Study well and behave."

"Yes, Mama," they chorused, calming somewhat. Then they ran outside with school backpacks, apparently on their way to school.

I had assumed long ago that in my dream, the yellow house was in South America, and the language being spoken was Spanish. But God had given me a dream of my future before I knew what it was or what it meant. It was clear now that the house was in Africa, and the language was French. Who knew what the call on the lives of the children would be? That was not something to be worried about. After all, things had come to fruition without me remembering the dream and even getting some details wrong. It was a striking revelation for me, and the more I mused over it, the more God's power to control our world began to sink in.

During the ceremony, I shared my childhood dream and present-day realization with the audience, encouraging them not to be discouraged by circumstances but to trust God with their lives to fulfill His purpose, whether they understood the details or not.

I had come to the ceremony feeling sad that my move to Ethiopia had prevented me from spending more time on-site at the DRC project. I left very encouraged that my presence was unnecessary for God to complete the planned work. He had all of the pieces worked out. One of the pieces was one of Papa's interpreters from my first visit to Nkamba. He had come to Kinshasa after the church split, and we kept in touch through this tumult. Unbeknownst to me, he had returned to school and now had the degree to coordinate the projects. Other people's names had come up for the same, but they had been clouded by questionable activity. His academic efforts and continued commitment to service and transparency impressed me when we discussed the project. He was the right man at the right place. He was humble and wise in solving problems.

We had heard of parents dropping their children off at caring orphanages for a few years and returning to claim them. They intended to have someone raise the child until they were old enough to bring them a profit. This was done mainly in the case of girls, who would be reclaimed just in time to be exchanged in marriage for the bride price paid by a willing husband. We did not want to fall victim to such a cruel scheme. So, we decided to accept only children legally declared state wards. It seemed like a long wait for the process of identifying such children. In the countries I visited, skipping a daily meal or two at my hotel would amount to a sizable donation of money to a local orphanage for food or other needs. I continued this practice until Evelyn's Arms Orphanage received our first baby.

In the meantime, we focused our DRC activities on the widows' training classes. In two years, we had over seventy-five widows graduate from our training. We required proof of qualification to ensure we addressed the needs of actual widows. Making paper records a requirement in a country where death records were not consistently issued was challenging. Many of the women could not return to their former homes to ask for available copies. People were often buried on family farms without official papers. So, we made a list of the acceptable substitutes.

Another stipulation was that our program's widows must have at least one child under six. This allowed us to provide support to widows at risk of losing their children to street gang life.

Unfortunately, we had not considered what these young children would do while their mothers were in class. Once the mothers asked this question, we knew this was an opportunity to train the children and the mothers. We were compelled to start a preschool and early primary school. No payment was charged to the mothers enrolled in the training program. At the same time, we expected the women to earn enough money after our training program to pay for continuing their children's education. This school expanded when women completed our training program after six months and wanted their children to complete the school year, which spanned nine months. As an incentive to apply the skills learned, we agreed to let them pay for the additional three months with a token amount or with in-kind labor. Within a short time, the surrounding community requested admission for their children. Our school charged the lowest fees and offered a special rate for widows whose children were not currently in our program.

The project manager was honest and kind-hearted. I am grateful for his insight and input on the project's implementation. Working with and explaining to him, he learned more efficient business operations and developed some practical applications. The project would have to succeed by benefiting those in need, the nonprofessional and uneducated. This required a cultural and moral point of view. It was reassuring knowing he was in charge. I lived in Ethiopia and traveled a lot.

My health improvement work and efforts continued in Ethiopia. My travel schedule sometimes required me to fly to a different country every two weeks for two months, which allowed me to use the program's travel funds more effectively and efficiently. These were the initial years, and I carefully worked closely with the Geneva team to build a solid program base.

It was unclear about what I should do for the orphanage and women's training program. How was I supposed to fulfill my life's calling standing in the hall of the big yellow house if I was not even in the country?

I complained to a friend about my situation on a particularly frustrating day. In tears, I whined, "I don't see how I'm supposed to move forward when I don't know the direction to head in. I keep heading toward daylight, only to find a single bulb leading down another long, dark hall. I don't know the next step."

He laughed and said, "How fortunate you are. You don't have your ingrained ideas of what to do. So, you are straining to hear what God is telling you. With that attitude, you can't go wrong. The ones who get lost are the ones who think they know the way and walk off cliffs with confidence. You keep asking God to guide you. You can't go wrong doing that."

That message struck my core. I started replacing my complaints with questions and prayers about the next steps. I remembered a message about God's word being a lamp and a light. A lamp was for close work, for each footstep to avoid stumbling. A light provided a broad-range, undetailed assurance that we were on track to the intended destination ahead. There were periods when I knew exactly where to put my foot next. I had no idea at other times and stood still in my mind. It was like marching in place.

***

Telling stories of my experiences helped pass the time as I spent many hours traveling within and between countries. In Ethiopia, a driver loved to hear my stories about my life lessons and beliefs. He asked me to write them down so he could share them with his children and friends. He complained that by the time he got home, he had remembered only a few of the details that had made the story so engaging.

As a child, I often sat in church or at home with guests as my dad told stories more impactful than Aesop's fables. Each story was meant to be a lesson. He conveyed it with sounds and expressions, making the action come to life. It was better than TV. People would roar with laughter or sit in quiet reflection, digesting how the story applied to their lives.

Carrying on with my family tradition, I enjoyed telling interactive stories. Writing seemed too much work. I made so many work reports that my fingers were sore from typing. During college, short inspirational stories and skits for the church occupied my time when I was not working. I promised the driver that he would be the first to get a copy if I had the time to write the stories and get them printed.

I mentioned this promise to my friend in the women's ministry at the church in Addis Ababa. She encouraged me to find out what it would take to get such a book published. A few months later, I was excited to hold my first book, a collection of stories about the events in my life that had taught me lessons. Everyone who read the stories loved them.

Hoping to sell these as a fundraising effort and an inspiration, I spent a lot on postage to get them into the hands of people in the US who said they had a market. This could be the ongoing revenue source for the DRC project for years. One by one, my 'distributors' wrote back with reports that no books were sold, and not even the postage was recovered. This was a disappointing period of apparent failure.

During the same months, my investigation into creating a second album of songs led to a worship leader at a large church in the area. We agreed to begin work on an album of songs I had written. Despite many challenges and obligations, we emerged with a lovely album that has ministered to many worldwide. Unfortunately, not many of them sold. The cost was recovered, but no project funding materialized. What was I missing?

Chapter 19

My job at WHO provided enough financial support for the DRC project to continue. However, one troubling thought gnawed at the back of my mind. There was a significant gap between my mandatory WHO retirement in five years and the eighteen years it would take to raise a child. Where was the support money going to come from in the meantime?

Known as an idea person, it was disappointing that my ideas had worked for many others but were unsuccessful in developing fundraising streams for the DRC projects. I was at a dead end. When I shared my concerns with my mom, she sent me encouragement from Galatians 6:9 (LEB): "And let us not grow weary of doing good, for at the proper time we will reap a harvest, if we do not give up."

How was I supposed to know when the proper time arrived? Why wasn't it hurrying up? Instead of an answer, there was a question. "How can you be so hurried when you don't know where you are going? Can you focus on what you know and can see to do?" So, I focused on where I was and those God had surrounded me with.

I learned about the Kimbanguist church community and relationships rule through the church's traditions and celebrations. One tradition is the practice of annual self-accountability. Once per year, before the year ends, each member is supposed to identify people they have been offended by or think have offended them. These people are to be contacted, and all possible efforts are to be taken to make amends with them. I studied the importance of forgiveness in my home church and tried to forgive offenses against me very quickly. I had a long-standing habit of reviewing the day's activities and calling people if I had a question for them or a possible misunderstanding between us. I thought no one in the world could have something against me, but the more I thought about the subject, the more one person stood out as likely to have a grievance against me.

For years, I had thought very rarely of my former husband. He had divorced me because I would not submit to his demand to cover up the visa application for his mistress. Among other things, he'd sworn to ensure I did not finish medical school. I would speak to him only when necessary to avoid arguments or hearing hateful or hurtful words. I also strove to avoid negative statements when mentioning him to others, especially my children. Then, once our children were adults, there was no reason to maintain contact with him.

Wanting a clean spiritual slate with no doubt hanging over anything, I wondered how to approach the issue of making amends with my former husband as painlessly as possible. I ruminated over this for days, and I finally realized that my primary focus in all this should not be to avoid pain. My goal was to rid my heart of any possible interference with my relationship with God. I had not hesitated to ask my former husband for forgiveness for everything I could think of. At least, that's what I felt from my point of view. I did not believe he would ask for forgiveness for his offenses against me. Anyway, I had forgiven them long ago but had not informed him. Sighing, I called my son to get his father's number. He was surprised, so I told him why. He warned me not to expect anything positive. I laughed and told him my hopes were not high for that. This was for my benefit in obedience to God.

He gave me the number, and I called. My confidence ebbed with each unanswered ring. I was about to hang up when I heard his voice. "Hello?"

Trying to sound cheery, I said, "Hi, this is Joyce."

"Joyce?" he paused. "It's been a long time. What's wrong?"

"Nothing's wrong, and I won't keep you long. I'm just following a tradition in my African church. This call is to let you know that I hold nothing against you. We start right now with a clean slate. If you need help with something, you can call to see if I can help." There was silence, which I expected to be followed by cursing and outrage.

He surprised me by softly saying, "You were always such a good-hearted person . . . Yes. It's a good idea to mend our fences."

This caught me entirely off guard, and his words delighted me. It seemed an easy win. "Great. That's all I wanted to say. Thanks. Goodbye," I said, ready to hang up.

Then he added, "Wait, there is perhaps one thing you could help me with." My heart sank as warning bells went off in my brain, and I wondered what he would say. Mental sirens blared, and danger lights flashed. "I hear it's pretty easy to get diamonds and gold in Zaire. Can you give me some contacts to work with?"

This had an easy response. "Unfortunately, when arriving in the DRC, I committed to have no engagement in gold or diamond dealings. So, no, I do not run in those circles."

He ignored my words and insisted that there must be somebody I knew who did. I said I'd pass on his contact information if I heard of someone. This appeased him, and I hung up. Staring at the wall, I reflected sadly on his seemingly unchanged attitude. Only God knew his heart.

Admittedly, I had probably acted the same way toward God. He'd offered me forgiveness fall after fall. Was I sincerely grateful enough to ask Him to keep me from falling so frequently? Was I guilty of rushing to the next thing I wanted Him to give me or for which I needed His help?

I whispered, "God, I want to be more grateful to you. Help me see each time you forgive me as an opportunity to change as an offering of thanks. May a cry of gratitude, pure and simple, be my response." The image of a clean, blank page of that account appeared on the wall. A smile spread across my face as a great weight was lifted off of me. My part in mending a tattered and marred relationship was done. I was free. The rest was between God and him.

***

Fortunately, Ethiopia had one of our country's focus partnerships, but the hospital was far from Addis Ababa, where I lived and took my many flights. I proposed collaborative programs with other agencies that expanded our ability to achieve mutual goals. We increased the number of people trained on the same day by working together on agreed-upon topic areas and materials. It sometimes made for a long day, but the attendees received two certificates and spent less time away from work. It was indeed a win-win-win result. More training was planned, and I began writing a report on the benefits of this type of collaboration. Then the notice came.

Unaware that plans for my life had been under discussion, the notice of this decision was unexpected: My base station was being changed to Zimbabwe. This was a strategic positioning to move me from the limited coverage of a country office to a sub-regional office for twenty-three countries. I would promote health safety through training, consulting on revising national health policy, and medical school training curricula.

This was a tremendous promotion and should have caused me elation. I would no longer be an outsider managing a superimposed Geneva-based project. However, I was unsettled because of what I had experienced in the DRC. People were often given positions or titles without a salary or a working budget to develop or implement plans. The funds for my central WHO project were only to be used for countries with hospital partnerships. Money for other projects was also explicitly funded. Were the deciders aware of this? How were the activities in the rest of the countries to be paid for? My questions were answered with a report for duty date confirmation and a request for a two-year budget proposal. This was comforting, and my preparation for the move began.

I said goodbye to my friends, fellow church members, and work colleagues, who saw this as a big promotion. It felt like another uprooting, with parts of my stability and spiritual resources ripped away. It also posed an additional hurdle to visiting the DRC. God knew all this and would provide an even better place to thrive. Nevertheless, it was painful to leave Ethiopia.

***

In 2011, I moved to a hotel in Harare, the capital of Zimbabwe. Most of my time was spent outside the country, supervising the efforts of the eleven countries now in our priority program. I had not found a church that held English-speaking services to attend during my rare weekends in Harare. One evening, on a phone update, my aunt and uncle mentioned that their home church was associated with an African church in Zimbabwe. Excited when my aunt gave me the phone contact of the pastor's wife, I called immediately and left a message. Imagine my surprise when I discovered the services were held in my hotel's auditorium. How had the answer to my prayer been only an elevator ride away for all of this time? My meeting with the pastor's wife after service began an exciting church engagement and contribution.

Although traveling considerably for the Geneva project. I immersed myself in church activities and became dear friends with associate pastors. My church participation included writing study books about personal spiritual growth and teaching women's physical health classes for the church. I joined a small church group where we shared insights and encouraged each other through different life situations. My activities included support for the ministries for young people, women, and men with the study books produced, classes, and discussions. For a short time, my singing talent allowed me to become part of a worship training program's choir, sponsoring an annual training for African church worship teams. My spirit thrived, enjoying rich and fortifying food.

If Ethiopia had been a high-flamed, rolling boil period in my life, Zimbabwe was a low-flamed, constant simmer requiring frequent stirring to avoid bottom scorching. The WHO Geneva project's tools and experiences have been used in our new and associated countries. Our team's efforts yielded great results, which the international health community recognized and appreciated. We were granted extended funding and additional countries with activities. Our hospital partnership countries were committed, eager to succeed, and grateful.

***

Outside of church and work, I discovered a small children's home for orphans, visited it, and left a donation. Arranged in "family" groups, children of various ages lived in a home environment with a "mother" or caregiver who prepared their meals. The family living

168

structure provided loving care and discipline. It was a different arrangement than I had seen before, a mixture of a foster home and an orphanage. Several houses had been built, and more were planned on their extensive land. Impressed by the orderliness and home environment created, I visited and donated again.

The third time, I was given a grand tour. There was a large garden area where most of their food was grown. The community had recently helped build small classrooms. After school, these rooms provided a safe place for the community's children to do homework activities and be tutored. It endeared the children's home to the community, grafting it into the area's culture. During the day, the rooms served as classrooms for the resident orphans' school. They did not have to attend schools far away or pay the tuition usually required for primary school.

A church/auditorium building had been constructed to serve as an auditorium for the children's home and school, where town meetings, weddings, and other social events could be held. Any vegetables in excess from the garden, blankets, or home goods received as donations were sold to the surrounding community's members at low prices.

The children's home had begun in 1960 with a pastor's efforts to provide orphaned and at-risk children with a warm, safe place to stay at night. He could not feed the gathered number until his church started to support the project. They gradually added aspects like a center to help those children suffering from psychological trauma or with special needs. It was inspiring to see the results of one man's initial efforts. I hoped that our DRC project would grow to be an integral part of its surrounding community and goodwill. I donated to encourage them.

It was unexpected when the children's home administration requested that I meet with them at my hotel. A group of three came: the church pastor and the children's home director with his wife. They asked why I visited and donated to the children's home. I explained my heart's dream to rescue the DRC's children from being condemned to life on the streets. The director then told me the incredible story of his life.

He had endured enough harsh and unfair treatment to fill a book. Tears filled my eyes several times as he spoke. There was an important thing he did as he told his moving story. In every heart-rending, hopeless situation he had gone through, he carefully pointed out the people he realized God had placed at the right time to show him loving kindness and provision. His was a praise story of God's faithfulness. It is one thing to say that God has answered prayer faithfully. However, recognizing when you didn't pray for something and God helped you is another. God had used strangers to fill his needs in unimaginable ways. God had kept him safe despite his early childhood betrayal and abandonment by his parents, verbal and emotional abuse by relatives and classmates, and suffering as a victim of planned harm and humiliation.

He had grown into a generous, kind, and empathetic man, willing to help others despite personal economic loss. God sent people and opportunities to help him at strategic moments. He had started picking cotton at five to have enough to eat and could not attend primary school for years. He was now well respected, with graduate degrees, and reaching out to help those in situations like those from his past. God continues to bless him. He became one of my life's heroes.

Inspired to recognize and point out God's merciful hand in my life as he had done, I encouraged him to write his story as an inspiration to others and offered to ghostwrite it. Unfortunately, he soon left, accepting a national children's home director job in another country. Our lives crossed only briefly. It was long enough for me to hear what I needed to help avoid growing weary in my work for orphanages.

Although it was not one of our specified countries for the Geneva grant, working in the subregion office gave me access to Harare's city hospitals and the Ministry of Health to do training and help advise on national patient safety policy. My focus included making the success of our project available to the over forty remaining countries, which meant developing tools for their use.

The first tool created was a fill-in-the-blank national policy outline. This form outlined the main objectives of each hospital safety program. All possibilities seen in other countries were included as possible options to be selected. Each section had flexibility, allowing for local needs and resources. No country needed to start from scratch. It was adaptable for any country's health ministry, regardless of size and the issues they prioritize, and aimed to develop their implementation activities and budget plan. Life was good, with me working smarter and not harder.

***

I continued writing novels with the full intention of having them published to raise money for the DRC orphanage. An agent needed to do the legwork for me, including giving me updates on the book's publishing, marketing, and other things. In my limited research and phone calls, many smooth-talking salespeople offered to make my publishing dreams come true. I had to remind myself that they wanted to help their company realize their dreams, not mine. Who could I trust?

There were other options. I could invest in publishing the books myself, keeping all the income for the orphanage. They would have to be printed in the States and be of far better quality than the ones printed in Ethiopia. I would need an expert to work all of that out. There was also the option of music. I had written songs since college, often singing them to myself as worship or encouragement. Some of those were used to complete two albums. If someone in the States was willing to work with me, we could use some others to make new albums. How could I find them?

Chapter 20

Mali

One of my extended training and consulting trips took me to Ghana. I met with the national officials there to prioritize the focus points in the country's health safety policy. On the second day, I received an urgent call from Geneva asking me to make a quick side trip to Mali. A team of international consultants was setting up measures to prevent Ebola cases from crossing the border Mali shared with Guinea. Guinea was experiencing an epidemic of Ebola cases with a risk of becoming a pandemic center. They soon realized there was no infection prevention and control expert. They requested that Geneva send someone immediately, as the group would depart in three days.

I was the closest geographically, and the request came from a French-speaking country in my region. Mali also happened to be one of my partnership project countries. So, Geneva assigned me to contribute to the team's creation of a national prevention plan. With the strategy of finding out what had been done and filling in any holes, I arrived early the following day and reported to the WHO country office.

There was little time to research resource needs outside Bamako, the capital city of Mali. But it had the densest population and, thus, the most lives at risk. After working with the expert team, I worked with the country office team. We drafted a plan to educate the healthcare staff on hand hygiene and preventing disease from spreading through contact. They would then train the staff in clinics and health posts. An immediate order was made for personal protective equipment (PPE) supplies. The rollout was to start in Bamako and spread to the land borders with less population and entry volume. All this would be in tandem with the international team's rollout plan to prevent the entry spread through airports and official immigration points. Unfortunately, we realized too late a vital issue had not been considered. The national borders were porous and poorly guarded. Families and friends passed back and forth across the borderlines as if they did not exist. These invisible lines had been established by politically powerful people living far away and had no impact on their daily lives.

A tired yet committed grandmother crossed the Guinea border on the eastern side of Mali. She took a public bus to her home, which was at a significant distance on the western side of Mali. She was traveling with her grandchildren, one of them sick. The ill child died shortly after they arrived. Public health alarms went off, and forensic teams were sent to investigate. Late in the afternoon on the day of my arrival, Mali's first Ebola case was confirmed. Our intense strategic planning session shifted from infection prevention to infection management. My plan to return to Ghana was canceled. All my clothes and materials were left in a now inaccessible hotel. The epidemic control team would be staying in the country for an indeterminate amount of time. This was no longer a drill. We were at war.

My supervisor in Geneva was informed that a hold had to be placed on my scheduled future activity outside Mali. In addition, because of the change in country status, there was a desperate need for at least two additional experts in infection prevention and control, training, programming, and evaluation. The local office worked to arrange a massive training session, but we needed help with assessment and follow-up. The borders and entry points needed urgent PPE protocol. Others would fan out nationwide to train all other healthcare workers. Geneva scavenged to find two volunteers in record time. It is still baffling how we got such a mountain of tasks done so quickly.

The two consultant experts arrived within a few days, and we divided the work after mapping out the overall plan. We detailed the strategy, roll-out sequence, equipment, and training team for the job. After the train-the-trainer session, we had people with the knowledge to provide expertise in each district. Working with the country office staff, the two new expert co-leaders would replace me.

After being replaced by the two new experts, I resumed my duties of building health safety capacity in other countries. Fortunately, no other Ebola cases were reported in Mali. I had escaped Ebola and breathed a sigh of relief as I could return to less dangerous places and situations until my retirement.

***

Subregional countries started hearing about the patient safety program. They requested training, tools, and policy development support. My department approved my proposed budget for help in three countries. But there was one misunderstanding after another. The bottom line was that there were no funds to do anything outside Harare and the countries covered by the grant. With my retirement date looming, I worked tirelessly to complete the implementation phase of Geneva program activities. Evaluation and follow-up remained. I had hoped I could train someone to replace me and devote time to subregional work.

The idea that the last months of my service to WHO would be fruitless was frustrating, but I refused to fade away without a fight. We held hospital sponsor training in Harare. Two of the largest hospitals tried an intra-country partnership as a model for future activity. We spent many days with the health ministry explaining the available tools. I set up video and telephone conferences to speak to countries about our tools and collaborated with other Geneva safety programs for surgery and childbirth.

In the evenings, most of my time was spent trying to hear God's solution to being blocked from travel because of the lack of funds. Hearing disappointing silence meant staying still. My complaints were reduced, and my work on church activities and projects increased. My retirement was a few months away. A feeling of expectancy caused me to work feverishly to tie any loose ends. There were rumors of the horrors of the worsening Ebola outbreak.

The Ebola outbreak in Guinea was limited to the one reported case in Mali. However, the disease had spread its tentacles of death to Liberia and Sierra Leone, two other bordering countries. As a result, it was declared a pandemic, and fear spread across the globe. Flights to and from the three affected countries were canceled, reducing the possibility of help arriving in the form of skills, equipment, or medications. The fear of exposure was overwhelming and produced chaos until logical heads prevailed, and this blockade was lifted. The number of deaths continued to rise.

In the face of Ebola's rapid spread, the WHO African Regional Office required officers to rotate in one of the three affected countries for six weeks. The three affected country offices were overwhelmed and understandably needed support. Few, including me, wanted to go. Ebola is a viral disease. It causes an agonizing death and, during its course, puts all of your loved ones, friends, and colleagues at risk. My days were filled with a busy schedule of trying to prevent annual epidemics and health risks in Harare and waiting for the requisite funds to travel to other countries.

After two additional months of waiting, it was clear that the said funds would not be available soon. So, it seemed a good time to get my six-week obligation for Ebola duty out of the way. I would get this obligation done so that it would not cause an unexpected interruption later. Guinea expressed an intense need for support. It was the only French-speaking country among the three severely affected, so my help would be the most useful there. What could happen in six weeks?

Chapter 21

The WHO office driver from Conakry, Guinea, met me at the airport and drove me to my hotel. It was exciting to look out the windows and ask questions. With only six short weeks ahead, I was determined to make the most of every moment. Not knowing the city's layout, I asked to visit the country office first, only to learn it was conveniently located on the same road as the hotel.

At the office, I learned that before I could start any work, human resources had to issue me with an official ID and complete my registration. The process dragged on longer than I'd anticipated, but I was relieved when it was finally done—I was now officially part of the country office staff. My first act was to make an appointment to present myself to the WHO country head the following day. Running back downstairs to the human resources office, my next act was to locate the Infection Prevention and Control Team leader. The official looked at me with a puzzled frown, and his answer took my breath away: "There is no team."

Thinking he was unfamiliar with the term, I wondered how it could be said differently. *Wasn't Ebola an infection whose spread needed to be controlled and prevented?*

My panic must have shown on my face. He quickly added that a local officer was responsible for hand hygiene and would have more information. I numbly went to see him, hoping things were not as bleak as they seemed. The officer explained he was assigned to cover the activity but had no training or experience. As far as he knew, I was the only WHO officer in the country with the expertise to do anything on the topic.

"Okay then. What is the national plan, and who is in charge?" I asked.

He shrugged. "I don't know of a plan. Isn't that why you are here?"

This time, stunned was not a strong enough word for the feeling spreading from the pit of my stomach through my heart to my brain. My face must have reflected my heart's turmoil, and I watched fear spread over his face before he diverted his gaze. He fumbled for his phone and said he was calling a representative of the Ministry of Health to see if they had a plan and would meet with me. We set up a meeting, and I walked out feeling hollow. *What was I overlooking or not understanding about the situation?*

Just a few blocks from the WHO office, my hotel turned out to be a surprising luxury—on par with an international five-star. After checking in and settling my things in my room, I returned to the lobby, went through the side door, and sat on the poolside terrace. The pool looked cool and refreshing as pleasant music played overhead. People sat sunning themselves with iced drinks beside them. A few yards away was an immaculate beach hosting coconut palms swaying in a gentle ocean breeze. It was hard to believe that so much horror and death lay not far away. The scene gave me a sensation of something familiar that I could not identify initially. Then, an idea struck me.

It felt like a holodeck—a simulated, three-dimensional environment designed for escape. The concept, which I'd first encountered on a TV show, allows people to temporarily step away from their realities and immerse themselves in another world without leaving the room. Today, actual holodecks exist in some universities in the USA. But I hadn't come to Guinea for an escape, luxurious or otherwise. I decided to find a safer, more modest place to stay. With only six weeks ahead of me, I needed to spend as much time as possible understanding the reality on the ground. At every turn, there was possible exposure to a disease that could kill me. I walked back to the office in search of more information. However, the officer I had spoken to previously had gone for Muslim prayers and possibly a late lunch. There was no idea of the time of his return.

During the brisk walk back to the hotel, I came across children with machetes who offered, for a meager price, to take a newly harvested coconut, chop off the outer shell, and hack a hole to allow me to drink the water inside. Far from clearing my thoughts, this only deepened my concern that things were even worse than I had imagined. These poor babies knew nothing about hand hygiene to protect themselves. They were trying to get money to take the edge off of the gnawing pain in their bellies.

I walked faster, trying to arrive before the tears could start pouring out. If the tears began, there would be no way to stop them.

My chest burned as I hurried straight up to my room. Once safe inside the door, I called my section head in Geneva and told him about the situation. Disappointed, hot, and tired, I immediately recommended my return to Harare. "How can I possibly do anything worthwhile in six weeks? It's like knowing you must clean out your refrigerator, but you only have enough time to empty everything onto the kitchen counter. It would only make things worse."

"You're the ideas person. Why not start by making a plan with a list of needs?" he countered. His advice was wise. "At least, whoever comes afterward can continue from there."

"You're right. I can at least do that," I agreed. "But I could have done that from Harare. It's so sad. People are dying from an infectious disease spread by contact and easily avoidable. I learned today that no PPE has been ordered because there is no money. Each organization orders stock for its staff. Someone has got to have money for something so simple."

"Yeah, it's unfortunate. How long would you need to finish the job? From your example, how long would it take to clean the refrigerator and get everything orderly back inside?"

"At least three months. It depends on the cooperation we get from those in charge and access to supplies, but I'll be retiring in July anyway. I can't do anything after that."

"July, huh? That's only four more months. I know it's not why you were hired, but it would have made sense for you to have gone there last year when all of this started." He sighed. "Okay. You work on the plan and send me a copy. I'll see if I can extend your stay beyond the six weeks."

"Okay, bye. I need to collect some information. I'll send you an outline this weekend."

"That's the spirit. Bye."

Admittedly, my spirits were already lifted at the end of the call. Planning was one of my talents, and I started listing the needed information. I hoped the health representative would help at our meeting tomorrow. In the meantime, a priority would have to be placed on establishing a team willing to stay longer than six weeks. If I stayed, having to train a new group every six weeks would not be an efficient approach. I could assign appropriate tasks to a stable team with identified strengths.

Most of all, funds were needed. The WHO country office had already clarified that they had no funds to fight the disease or prevent its spread. They reminded me that the WHO's role was to supply expert consultants. There were nonprofits in the country, and I should consider collaborating with them for projects needing funds.

I heard a meeting was held each morning to update data that all the important people from international groups and national leaders attended. I arrived full of hope, but as the meeting ended, I sat in confusion. I wondered again why it felt like I was missing an important key to success. The method to achieve success seemed so clear. My comments were not seriously taken into consideration. I had no explanation as to why this was so. From what I could glean, we had exceptional data collection, but no prevention strategy was in place or being developed. Perhaps the individual organizations were carrying out their plans, but there was no forum for us to share and possibly collaborate on our efforts. The collected data documented the increase in cases. The healthcare staff and their patients were still being infected, counted, and dying. If there was a prevention intervention plan, it was not well known.

After several days of attending these daily morning meetings, we received a report about two hospital workers from the large hospital down the street. Both had recently become infected, and sadly, one had passed away at home. Feeling a strong sense of urgency, I decided to ask the group for funds to support infection prevention. We needed money to buy PPE and equipment and to train staff and medical personnel at this large hospital nearby. The national director promised to look into my request. His answer gave me no hope and seemed to be a way of deflecting my request. Being successfully discouraged, I returned to my seat. At the meeting's end, there were a few comments about my courage to speak the truth for effective intervention. No one gave me words of hope or an offer of funds.

There was no hint that someone with money was listening until I received a summons from my country office head a few days later. He said the US had asked him to submit a proposal for eradicating

Ebola from the country. He didn't have many details regarding monetary limits, areas to be covered, or other limitations, but I could contact them directly with any questions. When I met with them, they expressed interest in a broad coverage plan to irradicate Ebola from the country. So, I gathered as much information as possible about needed materials and shipping prices, healthcare facility staffing training, and capacity and designed a detailed and stepwise itemized nationwide implementation program. The strategy, starting with the larger hospitals and stock depots, was built on national assumptions of the activities. That aspect was necessary to allow for completion even though implementing it would take longer than the four months remaining on my WHO contract.

I was surprised to find I had made the mistake of taking simple things for granted. When patients arrived at the top ten national hospitals, they walked in and waited in the crowd until their turn came. There was no input from medical staff, triage area, or vital sign measurements, including temperature or isolation spaces. This alone would have explained the majority of hospital outbreaks and healthcare worker transmissions.

I frontloaded the planned activities to ensure a national infection prevention capacity foundation. It would cost millions of dollars but would be exhaustive. No place in the country would be without the foundational knowledge to protect and control Ebola and almost any other contact-spread disease. They would have the equipment to apply this knowledge.

A call from Geneva brought unexpected news. An extension of my retirement date was authorized for an additional five months. The news was bittersweet. The extension was longer than I wanted, but it offered much-needed stability to our efforts. Working with a committed and talented team was an opportunity to significantly contribute to improving the world's health.

However, it meant that ten months of my life would be spent in the throes of fighting a murderous epidemic while building policies to prevent raging infections. This double load took a toll on my health at every level: spiritual, physical, and emotional. I was unwisely shouldering a heavy responsibility for the health of my sixteen core team members, even though it wasn't mine.

I had personally asked each core team member to stay and thought that was why they had agreed. Ensuring they took periodic breaks sometimes meant skipping my own. I checked each day's work every evening, knowing people's lives depended on it. I pushed, thinking it was necessary and possible, but I was wrong.

To my delight, some experienced volunteer infection prevention people had been in the country before I arrived. But they had been told there were no infection-prevention activities in place. They were very qualified but disheartened and had looked for other ways to spend their short volunteer term. Expert university professors accepted the assignment to work on developing the medical education curricula. Other team members came as volunteers from different organizations and were willing to be trained as trainers, evaluators, and report writers. Gradually, the team was building. Anyone who came for shorter periods was quickly plugged into the program structure with a specific task. My chest stopped burning. I was elated and put everyone to work.

I had not found an English-speaking church in this French-speaking country. It was difficult for me to translate my most intimate and passionate thoughts when I listened to the Bible being taught in French. My spiritual meals were from radio evangelists. My physical, emotional, and spiritual strength was ebbing just when I faced the most significant battle of my life. Distracted from my focus on the source of my strength, I learned firsthand the value of a fellowship of brothers and sisters with encouraging prayer partners. Long-distance phone calls seemed too expensive, and the time difference rarely made it convenient to call for prayer when I needed support.

As in most French-speaking African countries, Islam was the dominant religion in Guinea. Driving around the country as I was, I had not made friends outside the health battle zone. Friends and church members in the US and Zimbabwe were praying for me. But there was no one to sit with and discuss my spiritual battles. The need to be part of a church family had never been as evident as it was now for me since I saw the life-or-death importance of it every day in Guinea. A cold numbness began deep inside me. This was not fatigue caused by working too hard for too long; it was spiritual weariness. Spiritually speaking, it was not a safe place to be in. It was costly but did not have to be. It doesn't matter how strong you think you are spiritually. Your strength comes from your closeness to Jesus, the only direct source of strength, power, and endurance.

***

I had never been gone for so long and was worried about my luggage in the hotel storage in Zimbabwe. Would they rummage through my things, thinking them abandoned? I flew to Harare to find a solution using some of my accumulated vacation days. My assistant pastor friends agreed to store my stuff at their house, and everything was moved out of the hotel. This settled several problems. When I returned to leave for good, I could give them the things I did not want to take back to the States. They might like them or know of someone else who might. This would be the perfect unhurried chance to visit my friends.

It was also an opportunity to report verbally to the country office head. I wasn't sure if he knew my retirement date had been extended by five months.

After I explained what we had done in Guinea, he asked when they could expect my return to resume my duties for the sub-region. Several countries had requested my visit, and I wondered if the funds had ever come to carry out those duties. He promised to speak to the unit head when he returned from his present mission.

Chapter 22

California - Zimbabwe - Geneva

I arrived home after following a highly publicized event of Ebola exposure in the US. After landing at the airport and reaching the immigration port of entry, I joined the long line to pass in front of an immigration officer. As he reviewed my flight itinerary, his demeanor shifted. Nervously, he asked me to step away from the area. He pointed to a location near a distant wall marked by a yellow painted outline for me to stand and wait for an agent from the health department to escort me. I was about to ask how long it would take when a uniformed masked person approached me. The health agent greeted me, introduced herself, and led me to an isolated area.

Typical vital signs and ticking all the boxes in a negative symptoms checklist allowed me to enter the country under certain conditions. Being required to take my temperature and call my local health department with the results was a daily reminder of having been at risk of a deadly disease. Following protocols had kept me safe and prevented possibly exposing my family. I did not blame friends who called but were afraid to visit after discovering my present deployment.

I had left all of my clothes in Guinea to ensure I was not transporting anything potentially harmful, including Ebola. We did not know enough about the disease to offer a guarantee. We had followed the rules and protocols, and no one on my team or in the trained groups had been infected in Guinea. But the war was not over.

Despite the circumstances, I felt my spirit thawing and breathing again. I played with my two-week-old grandkids and enjoyed the warmth and love of my family. Too soon, it was time to return to the Ebola war zone. This time, however, my retirement date was four months away.

This was my hope and, at the same time, my problem. Now that the DRC project was thriving, it consumed a lot of money. Ninety percent of my monthly salary was spent on it, in addition to others' donations and the results of some fundraising. How was I going to collect enough money to keep it going?

***

Although we tried to keep a low profile, many political pressures weighed on us. Our success and large budget drew much adversarial activity and rhetoric.

The most significant impact we could make was concentrating our efforts on the ten university-associated hospitals and fully training the staff. We collaborated with sister groups to access money to build an emergency room with triage and isolation facilities at each site. We were happy our efforts brought about documentable improvements.

The first result in the data report was a striking decrease in infections among the healthcare staff. This was a relief, and we celebrated such encouraging news. Step-by-step PPE and hand sanitizer were made available, supporting our waves of training and safety practices. The ring immunization strategy, anthropology studies, and data about the location of cases combined to provide the much sought-after significant decrease in cases.

From all outward appearances, our team was on fire and setting unbelievable milestones. Not only were we training healthcare workers across the nation, but people from across the continent also came to our train-the-trainer sessions to take the expertise and documents back home to share. Years later, many who engaged with us were so empowered by our classes and the experience that they became national experts for patient safety when they returned home. This was not my aim, but it allowed me to impact Africa's health scenario positively.

We collaborated with everyone we could. The more the hands pushing the wagon, the easier it felt. The work friendships I developed locally were enriching. There was also vicious animosity. It had been naive of me to believe there was no place for politics in this peaceful effort to save lives. Politics was the deciding factor at the highest decision-making level, even at the expense of lives.

My last year as a full-time WHO employee allowed me to see aspects of international healthcare that were deeply disappointing, such as trampling on one another for credit or posturing for recognition. Was the childhood see-saw playground lesson to be confirmed as adults? At times, it seemed the power-heavy bully could place his weight and insist on suspending the efforts of others. At the same time, the year gave me some of my most significant medical career accomplishments and opportunities, deepest spiritual confirmations, and best friendships and collaborations. No situation or evil person can provide an excuse for failing to do right.

So, we worked hard to ensure no Ebola cases arose in hospitals or their surroundings. Then, we put our shoulders on the wheel with regard to the rest of the country. It was frustrating to have one or two cases reported just when we were days from declaring an end to the epidemic. International team members rushed to the area when a case was reported, using the entire arsenal of national experts and tools. There were door-to-door searches for hidden symptomatic people, immunizing those exposed, providing PPE, and teaching everyone the importance of hand hygiene. But we continued to have breakthrough cases. It was clear there was a hole in our armor. Despite our modern technology, our world experts were outmaneuvered by rural, poor, uneducated villagers. Groups of social anthropologists were sent in to live in these small village areas. It was apparent there was an intentional effort to hide the truth. Why? What did people hope to gain? The answers eluded us. What were we missing?

A ray of light broke through when a case appeared in the capital city, Conakry. A woman with fever and nausea presented to a main hospital campus after traveling in a crowded public bus from a distant rural area. A family member had advised her to go to the city and supplied her with finances for bus fare and food. The family member giving her the money was a prominent participant on the board for Ebola eradication. Why? What had made him do such a thing, knowing the risks?

He said it was to avoid the shame of an Ebola case occurring in his home area where he was in charge of Ebola eradication. He justified the intentional exposure to a fatal disease for at least a busload of his compatriots and hospital workers to avoid his village's public shame. There was another case in a small town where an older man died at home, and when the inspectors came, they found he had suffered from the widely publicized symptoms and signs of Ebola. Initially, no one answered why they had allowed the family and village to suffer such exposure. Finally, his oldest son reported they did not want their father to die in shame and be taken to a distant Ebola quarantine hospital to die alone. They had heard that family visits were not allowed for the inpatients with food or other comforts. He believed the community would blame them for not meeting their social responsibility and ostracize them for the rest of their lives. He also believed his father would haunt him for the rest of his life. There was no good in saving his life if he would be haunted and shamed by his community until he died. Avoiding this had been worth paying the ultimate cost.

Other stories reflected the same fear of shame, fear more important than death. A force more substantial than shame had to be identified to compel people in rural areas not to hide ill people or expose themselves or others to the disease. We looked at ourselves, the international community of volunteers who had rushed to fight the

Ebola war. Despite the sacrifice and risk of death, what compelled us? The team of anthropologists was given this information. We waited for any cultural tools they could provide to help as we fought with the scientific tools we had.

***

Another breakthrough case came when a village, under a lockdown and daily house-to-house searches, was found to have had yet another Ebola death. The following day, an unknown man appeared in town. When the authorities tried to arrest him for breaking the lockdown rule, he insisted he lived in one of the surrounding caves but was from the village. He then began to tell them startling stories about the many burials performed after dark to avoid being reported. He mentioned that during door-to-door searches by the medical team during the day, an ill person would be moved secretly to one of the houses already searched. The search conducted was very predictable, using the same daily pattern. This made it easy to evade detection. The medical team was speechless.

Authorities asked him why he had not been seen earlier nor registered as a town resident when the lockdown was implemented. He explained that he had separated himself as ordered by city officials to fulfill his duty as the village truthteller. He was not allowed to say anything false and kept the records for the town. To confirm his story, the elders were called upon. The group's demeanor changed when they entered the room and saw the truthteller was present. With great resignation, they confirmed what the truthteller had said. They were asked why they had done this. Did they not see their village had been dying one person at a time? Their explanation was they did not want the shame of being the last place in the country to have an Ebola case. They had rallied under the banner of false pride and lies. Their efforts to hide the truth in the shadows of night and webs of lies had had the opposite effect. They had thought they were avoiding shame. But pride is beneath the first layer of the threat of shame. It distorts our ability to think with logic or compassion. Our only hope is to find the truth tellers present worldwide and hear them before we all die from the hidden lies killing us.

***

With a renewed effort to work with the community and religious leaders, the national executive board leaders finally arrived at the countdown to Ebola eradication. Unfortunately, the final declaration date for the end of the pandemic in Guinea would come after I was obliged to return to the States. Harare was my required departure point, bringing me to the subregional office for a few days to close out my duty file and pack my bags. The staff kindly gave me a going-away party and a generous check for the children's home in Zimbabwe, the best gift ever.

We continued to support the women's cooperative formed by our trainees. However, the experts hired to teach follow-up business management skills failed to meet our expectations and left. The women overrode our advice to halt their activities until further support was found. The beginning of this gradual failure of the DRC women's cooperative occurred at a very stressful time for them.

At the same time, the fight for PPE in Guinea and wrestling for the right to claim the main role to success. There was also the imminent birth of my oldest son's twins. The DRC orphanage was expanding, and the newly started school was taking its first steps. I was hesitant to fly anywhere in light of the perceived risk of spreading the feared disease. The world's opinion coincided with mine, and no direct flights were available to most countries. The indirect flights to the States meant I would not arrive in time for the birth of my son's twins. Chaos swirled around me, engulfing the world. Finally, with two weeks left to declare Guinea Ebola-free, I had to be back in the US for an official retirement.

I heard about the possibility of working for WHO after retirement and applied for jobs as a consultant. Sometimes, this involved working in countries with a team of experts. Other times, it involved working alone using a template to collect information, make recommendations, and write comparative reports.

During the last assignments, I was concerned about the manager's frequent changes and the possible usefulness and quality of any results. My reputation stood for quality, and I did not want to lose my integrity by association. Although the only job available, I declined a further project with them. After nine years, I no longer worked for WHO. I was going home and needed a job.

Chapter 23

California

It was not clear what my next steps should or would be. I was responsible for the livelihoods of the two dozen families in the DRC, and this responsibility weighed heavily on my shoulders. For almost ten years, I flew worldwide, bringing answers, expertise, and options to countries, colleagues, and hospitals. I gave evidence-based recommendations and was armed with tools and encouraging stories of others' success.

I was home but not at home. There was no chauffeur to take me to my destination, worry about the car or fuel. There was no car, no house, and no job. My specialty board certification was the biggest problem I had not even considered. It had expired in the decade I had been out of the country. The process to qualify for the recertification exam required completing a project at a clinical practice, with patient data collection during treatment assessment. I tried to identify a clinic near home to do this without success. An unexpected option arose, allowing me to work at a clinic dear to my heart.

I grew up in a rural area where my dad served as the pastor of a small church. He dedicated himself to fighting for the community's access to essential social services such as early childhood education, clean water, and healthcare. He had died days after sustaining injuries in a car accident while on his way to a county planning meeting.

Friends and community members had named a small clinic after him to honor his memory and started a nonprofit organization that had undergone several changes. I was unaware until my brother told me about the five-clinic operation it had become. He explained its benefits to the entire area, extending hundreds of miles from the original clinic. He had become the chief medical officer. They needed doctors and agreed to let me conduct the research with patients who agreed to it.

In 2016, this job allowed me to reacquaint myself with the area, which had changed drastically. I met some former classmates, one of whom was my patient. Sadly, many of our erstwhile neighbors had died or moved away. The grass-covered hills had become a beautiful community, and time had brought other delightful changes. Each clinic I rotated through was distinct, reflecting the area it served. Easing back into clinical life was relatively easy. However, I did not intend to stay past the completion of my project toward being recertified.

The hotel they arranged for me to stay in was within walking distance of a familiar church. As a child, our church fourteen miles away would sometimes come to have joint services. No one from the old days was still there, but many new, wonderful people had created a joyful fellowship space, and I joined the church.

***

The orphanage section of the DRC project complex was named after my mother. My dream of how our orphans would feel was summed up in one expression: the peaceful one on the face of a child sitting or sleeping in her arms, convinced all was well. I have memories from all over the world of her comforting a crying baby, cranky toddler, or tearful young child. Children and plants responded like magic to her touch. Yet, she had the strongest character of any woman I have ever known. My mom was an ardent advocate for the DRC project and served as its secretary, treasurer, and fundraiser.

I once asked my mom if she had ever considered traveling to Africa. It was interesting to hear that during college, she had attended a speech by the president of Liberia. She had been so inspired that she'd decided to get a job and save enough to visit the country after finishing college. However, she had met my dad while looking for her first job and put all travel aside. I was glad she could visit several African countries during my sojourn and our medical missions. Through her, a friend would also touch the continent differently.

A couple of old friends reconnected with my mom. During my childhood, they had been members of our church when my dad was a chef and young minister. They arranged to meet my mom for lunch. I went along since I was Mom's chauffeur. They had much to update since the time their children played together while the adults had intense Bible discussions.

The woman turned the lunch conversation into my activity. I spoke about my medical duties and the call to the DRC project supporting orphans and widows. I told her of the children we hoped to rescue from a life on the street or worse. We had recently received a baby suffering from severe physical and neurological damage. Street children had found her abandoned, abused, and left for dead. She had lived, and the government had deemed us the organization to care for her with love.

Hearing about our work, my mother's friend was touched and began telling me about her work with young women in crisis pregnancies. It was encouraging to hear she had been so involved in helping young women consider all their options and to be reminded that God places someone to help people with all kinds of needs. She surprised me by asking for my photo and the address of our organization to send donations. The photo was to be put on her refrigerator door to remind her to pray for us every time she passed by it. She said she could not send much but would be consistent with prayer and a monthly check. She kept her word and, with each check, sent a Bible verse and words of encouragement. Her faithful gestures uplifted me on many days and inspired the women as they trained to care for their families. Her story and gifts of love were encouraging. The widow training program area was named after her as Muriel's Place.

***

My mother became very ill the year I retired. She had multiple ER visits while I was working at the clinics named in my dad's honor. It was disconcerting to me to see this vibrant woman, a spiritual and emotional pillar in my life, gradually becoming too frail to care for herself. While I was overseas, my siblings had arranged for her to stay at their homes. Now, because she wanted to stay in her own home, a caretaker was appointed to be with her during the day. When I returned after retiring from WHO, I worked as a consultant because the DRC orphans needed food and caregivers. I also wanted to spend as many evenings as possible with my children and grandchildren living in other cities. These things pulled in opposing directions, and I felt more than torn. It was more like being shredded.

It did not matter if I sat by her bedside for hours as she enjoyed the quietness or music. Being a light sleeper, she asked where I was going if my position changed slightly. I smiled, remembering sitting in church, thinking I was out of sight behind her, doing something or talking when I was not supposed to. I don't know how she could tell, but I would see her turn and stop me with one glance. She still had eyes in the back of her head.

Sometimes, unintentionally, we can be so self-centered. It's as if another person's life becomes significant only after they step into the spotlight of meeting us. The rest of who they are is left in the shadows, out of sight and mind. Truthfully, many have much wisdom and helpful experiences to share with us regarding what to avoid or search for. Their words could be a boost, helping us reach our destination or beyond. The length of their lives doesn't matter. The critical measure is quality. My mom had poured her life into excellent service to God. This was visible in her professional graph, with promotions to the top of her career stream. It was displayed in her parenting as she raised her children to be kind professionals in the form of a teacher, three medical doctors, and a lawyer. It was seen in the innumerable spiritual children she mentored and taught to strive for excellence. She constantly challenged others to do things better than they thought they could and go farther than they thought they would. This was apparent in the irrefutable richness of her life. Her actions, words, and deeds will continue to impact future generations.

Finally, she allowed us to clear out everything and put her house up for sale. She handed her items to those she intended to have them when they came. As much as possible, she could acknowledge her love for each and give a token of remembrance. I was so happy that she had done this peacefully and transparently. So, there was no fighting, no new arguing. She had also arranged her finances very clearly. She was able to spend time living with each of her three children in their own houses before entering a hospice. My youngest sister's house was where she stayed in her last days. The going-home celebration was just that, with the family there. She had previously given all her treasures to those she'd intended them for. The realtor was handling her house for sale. There were no arguments. Peace. What a lovely and delicately crafted gift she left us.

***

A combination of events was responsible for the final pieces falling into place, which led to my decision to leave the job of working in the clinics named after my dad. The disagreeable part of the week was flying home on weekends. How had I survived the years of constant flying for four to nine hours at a time? My WHO job had kept me thousands of miles away from my family. I was no longer thousands of miles away, but a distance of only hundreds of miles prevented me from seeing them now. My emotional debt to the world and my hometown's health was paid. I wanted to spend time with my family, and I left at the end of the year.

I took a two-month locum tenure position to earn money so the DRC project could function until enough monthly donation commitments were enrolled. After two months as a care unit staff member, I was asked to stay as service unit head. This was unexpected but very welcomed. Once again, I gave much of my salary to the DRC project and loved my job. My boss perfectly balanced attentiveness, excellence, and openness to creative professional ideas. The unit became more efficient and was expanding when the unexpected happened.

The massive wave of the COVID-19 pandemic in 2020 struck our healthcare system with such force that it nearly capsized. Many smaller clinics around us closed their doors, and even our organization had to scale back services in our regular clinics.

Our unit became the organization's default. All my strategic planning skills and flexibility were brought into play. We waged war with a deadly disease, but this time, it was not in a faraway country full of unknown people. This time, it was on home soil and for fellow citizens. Fortunately, my team of providers was committed and improved in confidence as they followed protocols and successfully served a hurting community.

Our efforts resulted in patient-seen tallies that surpassed expectations, making us proud of our contribution and the administration's support in overcoming supply shortages.

We were successful, but other changes were needed to improve our efficiency further and expand the number of patients seen. I submitted a detailed report. Because my recommendations were neither refuted nor accepted, I perceived this as a vote of no confidence. Life is too short to waste even minutes trying to convince anyone of the usefulness of my suggestions. After weeks of no answer or explanation, I resigned with three months' notice, offering to train my replacement. Unfortunately, one was not hired before I left.

I was sure that, during this time, a funding opportunity would present itself. While applying for jobs, I prayed and fasted. Was I supposed to return to the DRC and work from there? The project might gain more attention if I did so, leading to an improvement in the fundraising activity. Three story plots began to whirl in my mind, and I started writing as my thoughts brought out ideas and substories. These fell into three initial story plot groups, and I needed to figure out what to do with them. Soon, I was writing three novels at once and needed help to ensure they were successful.

***

My daughter and I had moved closer to my job, but we still drove two hours for the Sunday roundtrip to our church. Because of the distance, I felt excluded on many levels and wanted to be a part of a church in our community. My daughter and I had been listening on the car radio to a pastor whose church was twenty miles away. The first Sunday we visited, we fell in love with the warm environment, the movement of the spirit, and the ministries meeting so many points of need. We joined the church.

Wanting to become a more integral part of my new church, I thought the best way to do this would be to join a small group. I joined the writers' group sponsored by the church and was delighted to find such a thing, having never been to a church with a group for writers. Advised to attend writers' conferences, I learned years' worth of information in a short time.

A company asked me to allow a limited edit of two of my books, and after republishing, they began to sell. However, they did not raise significant funds. I wrote new short stories based on my experiences. I wrote stories for my grandchildren as gifts for birthdays and Christmas. These adventure stories included pictures of some of their favorite stuffed animals, toys, and daily activities, with a lesson-learned ending. This was encouraging, and my writing quality and exposure improved significantly. I am so grateful for all the help and advice from generous fellow writers. The books were written to encourage and inspire my fellow believers with the hope of raising money for the orphanage. Friends and relatives donated extraordinary amounts to the DRC project, including the church's women's Bible class. A friend bought my ticket to make the annual DRC visit. However, my concern about financial support for the DRC project continued to rise.

Rising inflation worldwide continued to drive the cost of our construction higher. The longer we took to buy the materials to finish the building, the higher the completion costs. We struggled to meet expenses as our donations decreased. At the same time, not finishing the building meant we couldn't increase the enrollment of students in the school and earn the fees to pay our teachers' salaries. We charged the lowest fees in the area and offered payment in kind. We also provided scholarships to community students, allowing them to further their education. However, we must think differently to create options to reduce the expenses of the DRC project.

Chapter 24

The Democratic Republic of the Congo

In February 2019, my uncle and long-time supporter flew with me for twelve thousand miles over two days on a historic journey to see the project as part of my annual visit. There was to be a celebration of this momentous occasion. The blue compound gate was flung open as the horn sounded to let the project coordinator drive us through in his jeep into the Solid Rock Youth Complex. Dancing women and singing children greeted our arrival.

I hesitated momentarily in my seat, remembering Dad's dedication to responding to the needs of the people around him as a young man. He had become a spiritual shepherd in a small rural canyon with a minority population, where he'd fought for adequate water supply, roads, services, and social justice on a nonpolitical battlefield.

Although he'd never run for public office, many of the highest-elected politicians in California at the time had attended his funeral. This was a testimony to the power of the love of God to tether someone's heart to a place and show His might. This quiet yet powerful example of service spurred my commitment to always do my best. My dad had died months before I'd set foot on the African continent. So, he'd never seen or heard about the many countries I'd visited or worked in. A moment of grief came with a thought that he had missed seeing the fruit of his example. Then, my heart swelled with joy and thanksgiving as the car door opened, and I turned to see my dad's younger brother smiling as he stood near me. I was happy thinking of my uncle being here with me today as a proxy for many.

It was not only my dad who came to mind. This uncle had played a starring role in my life story. He had lived with my mom and dad at the beginning of their marriage and in the early lives of my older sister, myself, and younger brother. He had been the one to scout out our move to California. My mother and older sister had died months before this visit, and he represented my entire American physical and spiritual family. A man in his eighties, he had never visited Africa before and had taken on the challenge with courage. I was also thankful that my uncle was a man of God, a bishop, and a pastor. An entire church jurisdiction in the States followed his progress and prayed for his mission's success and safe return. My uncle would testify to the power of God's hand to reach out through a poor man's family in the Southern United States to show His love for poor children in Central Africa.

This was the first time in over seven years that someone from the States had visited the project compound with me. The additional value of him being a man of God and a member of my family's elders was not lost on the community. Women who were former trainees rushed forward to stand beside us, dancing and singing a welcome as we exited the car. Our school students and orphans had lined the foyer of the building, and the teachers prompted them to burst into a song punctuated with rhythmic clapping. The leader called, and the rest sang in reply energetically as we mounted the stairs. The younger ones were so enthralled that they did not seem to hear anything. They stared at us wide-eyed, bumping into the others beside them.

We were led to sit at the head table in the dining hall, and the children filed in after us to occupy the arranged seats. I could feel the audience's eyes boring into the figure of my uncle. He was different than they had expected. I am sure, at first glance, they thought he had albinism. They watched his every move and were delighted when he spoke. He spent much of the next two days with them. His prayers left a profound impact as he took a tour of the three-story complex and the deep hole made for the foundation of the school building yards away.

On our last day visiting the complex, we went from one crowded classroom to the next, handing each student a package of cookies with a prayer. We had started with the preschool class and were tired when we returned to the main floor. My uncle was sitting and drinking a bottle of water at the bottom of the staircase leading to the top floor when something curious happened. One of our youngest orphans in the preschool was munching on some of the cookies. With unsure steps, he smiled and came over to stand beside my uncle, leaning against his leg. He looked up with a slight smile, enraptured by my uncle's eyes.

This might not seem exceptional on the surface. So, I will give some background. This little boy had earned the nickname "Prime Minister" because his expression was always stern. He rarely smiled or appeared at ease with strangers. But he was smiling and eating leisurely, leaning on a stranger's leg. They exchanged smiles, and although they did not have a language in common to communicate on a social level, this was a special moment. A deep sense of appreciation flowed between them, which could only have been of a spiritual nature, and I took pictures of them. A few minutes later, the special moment passed, and the gang of orphans descended the stairs. We took photos of the group, and he prayed for them.

Later, I explained the "Prime Minister" case to my uncle, who shared the photo with a few friends. Someone in the States put it online, and emails poured in about how it had touched them. They didn't know the story, but everyone felt the unique moment captured in the photo.

***

There was an unsettledness about what we would do in the remaining days before our departure flight. We had seen the project compound and the children. We had dined with the leading church officials I knew in town and met with former collaborators on various projects. We had visited local tourist attractions and did not want to waste the remaining time. When discussing this with my uncle, I found it funny that he had thought the same thing but had not known the options. A sudden thought came to me. We had a layover in Ethiopia. Maybe we could leave early for our return flight connection. I had a friend in the women's ministry at my old church that I had not seen or heard from for a while. Despite the short notice, she was happy to have us stay with her for two nights. The airlines had seats available, and we soon landed in Addis Ababa, unaware that God had several surprises in store for us.

We found my friend very ill and struggling to show us the hospitality she desired. More tired than I had ever seen her, she had overdone her preparations to welcome us into her home. Seeing her coughing and shortness of breath, we stopped her and prayed for her to be healed, and she started feeling better that night. The following day, she prepared breakfast and called for another taxi driver friend to take us for a reduced fee to various local places of interest. Leaving her to rest, we mapped out specific places to visit.

Over the next two days, we went on daytime trips to see the rich religious history of the churches carved out of rock and other ornate cathedrals, castles, museums, and burial grounds. I had not taken the time to see these when stationed there. No longer hurrying to complete a checklist between missions, my mind began to soak in Ethiopia's historic spiritual and worldwide political impact. We stood in the home of Haile Selassie, reviewed the documentation detailing Menilik's ties with Israel at the national museum, and saw technological innovations used by kings in the absence of electricity in palaces.

Lalibela was an inspiring testimony to the power of a life committed to following God's call. I had heard of this pious king who oversaw the hewing of churches out of solid rock in the western part of the country. The king had journeyed far away from home to establish one church near Addis Ababa. It was our once-in-a-lifetime chance to see an example of this unique structure type. When we arrived, the only visitors to the site during our tour, my uncle somehow developed a divine connection with the guide within minutes. We enjoyed a delightful time and were reminded of what God can do through people committed to His direction.

When we returned to my friend's home, we found a miraculous healing had occurred since our arrival. She was bright and cheerful and had energetically prepared a lovely traditional dinner of better quality than the food available at most local restaurants. She was a great cook anyway but had made a special effort since we were leaving soon.

She thanked my uncle for visiting and praying for her healing when she was in great need. He said God hears our prayers and heals us, and then he did something unexpected. After the final tea, he asked my friend if there was anything else he could do for her before we left. She laughed in surprise and said she had hesitated to ask for his help, but since he had asked, there was something. She had worried for a long time about her front room curtain, which had been taken down with the help of a friend to wash it. A temporary stationary curtain was flung into place over the bare front window. Unfortunately, it had rained that day, and her friend had gone home, leaving her without a way to let sunlight in during the day. The now dried unhung curtain lay over the back of the armchair with pins in place. As she lived alone, she was afraid to climb up the short ladder because of the risk of falling and being unable to call for help. Moreover, she had fallen sick.

My uncle laughed and said, "I don't plan on falling. Where's the ladder?"

Within minutes, he had restored things to normal. She clapped her hands with delight as she pulled on the cord to open and close the rehung curtains. She thanked him and said, "God knows our every need and meets us at that point to show His love."

We ended the day with joyful and thankful prayer. That night, I wrestled with questions. Why had God not seen the money for the construction of the school building as my need? Or had He? I was given the job to provide for the project's ongoing needs that would last years.

I could try to reduce costs somewhere to save for the construction. The architect complained again that a regular inflow of money was needed to purchase supplies and hire the crew. I didn't remind him again that our lack of funds had resulted from his failure to submit the grant proposal to the government on time. Friends and relatives showed up with outstanding support in the form of donations. We had fundraising campaigns and collected some money, but it never equaled the amount given from my monthly salary. That was not a present worry, I reassured myself. As long as my job continued, we would be all right.

Chapter 25

The Democratic Republic of the Congo

In the meantime, the DRC project's water access problem continued. We waited for years to pipe water to our side of the newly developing community. We decided to advance with our construction and greenhouse projects by paying for water to be piped to our property. We spent enormous amounts on permits, pipes, labor, and meter connections, which allowed intermittent water flow for only a few months. Then, it stopped completely when affluent and politically potent people began building their homes on the hillsides. They sent water trucks each morning to take all the water, leaving the people in our area without water to drink, cook, or bathe. The water we used came from rainwater stored in cisterns. This became a moot issue in 2022 when the fatal floods came. The soil instability resulting from unsafe construction on the hillsides and heavy rains caused flooding and massive mudslides. These washed away the water delivery system to the entire area. Many of the houses recently built were destroyed, and many lives were lost.

***

Electricity was also a long struggle—powerlines carrying electricity ended at the marketplace near the main road. Our DRC project was quite a distance beyond this point. The area was undeveloped, except for Catholic mission outposts for schools and clinics. The Catholic church provided these missions with generators and water wells.

The charge to build and manage a distribution unit or even to pay for access was beyond our means. However, we did make good use of solar batteries. We tried many ways to temporarily solve the problem of the lack of illumination at night. When we could afford it, we advanced to a system of roof solar panels. The panels were frequently blown off and damaged during storms. After years of waiting, the government brought the electricity cables to supply us with power. We had a joyful celebration for finally getting access to light during the night watch and thus securing the safety of the children and those watching them. It also helped the construction crew, who had previously rented a generator, to do parts of their work.

***

It was the usual time of year for my travel to the DRC, but I didn't have the money needed for transportation, lodging, food, and gas to move around town. Someone who knew I went at this time of year asked me about it. She offered to pay for my ticket when I said I had no money. I happily accepted the kind gift but explained my concern that we were not paying the staff. They had gone for months with only transportation money, and it seemed wrong to use so much money to travel there when we had not paid them. I promised to use the ticket if God made a way for me to go with the funds to clear their arrears. Maybe God was asking me to delay my trip this year or go the following year. I prayed and fasted. There were so many pieces to this puzzle. Believing I should prepare to go, I arranged for a place to lodge in. A friend in the DRC had told me that if I ever visited the DRC, I would be welcome to stay at their home. When I called, she agreed.

All that was missing was the money for the salary arrears. I refused to call or ask any specific person for a donation and prayed for God to lay it on people's hearts. *You, God, are my source. Arrange a resource you choose to provide what you know we need.* The women in my Bible study class generously raised money for half of a month's salaries. It was encouraging but far short of what was required. As time passed, I considered canceling my ticket to allow my friend a full refund and felt very discouraged. Because of a nudge from heaven, I got a call from someone who said they wanted to give a significant amount to the DRC project. It was more than enough for everything. Of course, it was. It came from God. It was the sign I had asked for. Things would run smoothly now because everything was in place. It signaled the falling apart of other pieces.

***

Despite careful planning, my visa was scheduled to arrive the morning of the night I was to fly out. However, if things did not go perfectly, it might come too late for me to make the first leg of a very tight itinerary. It was so stressful that I repeatedly reminded myself that too much prayer had gone into this and too many incredible answers had been received for this to fall through.

Three days before my departure, my DRC hosts called and canceled their invitation to lodge me due to a family emergency. I was tempted to be disappointed and angry . . .Then, in a flash, a thought sizzled through my brain. With no money for a hotel, this could only mean one thing. There had to be a much better place for me to stay in. It's the way God works. But where was it? I called around to other friends and found a room with meals at a lovely, better-secured, and logistically better-situated place for free. *That's how He works for His children.*

The DRC embassy processed my visa in record time. The weather allowed all the scheduled flights to run on time, and land connections were aligned to speed up the delivery. My visa arrived two days before my flight. In my experience, this was the best result I have ever seen.

I had told the coordinator not to tell anyone about my coming because I was not sure if I would have to change my ticket or try to scrape up money for a risky hotel room. But there I stood, ready to go, with everything in place. It was not how I'd expected, but it was much better. As shown by the Godly interventions, this was a divine commission. I could see God's hand moving on my behalf at every step. I saw what must always be happening behind the scenes as I sat smugly planning my journeys, unaware of the many things that could go wrong. Now that I had seen the details of God's intervention, could I ever take it for granted again?

Later, the coordinator said he'd told the staff they would have a special visitor without telling them who. I arrived to squeals of delight. Cheers roared when the coordinator announced he would start paying out the staff's salaries the next day.

After listening to reports from each departmental head privately, I realized that the most complicated cases were about those who still sided with a dismissed senior employee. They were convinced that the coordinator had abused his authority in dealings with him. I made sure I took them to meet with me and the coordinator to clear the air and agree on the steps forward. I decided to return the following weekday to talk in more detail with one person, but they declined, stating it was their day off. I found this odd since my limited available time was well known. We arranged to meet before my departure.

The following weekday, during a meeting in the coordinator's office, we were interrupted by a lot of yelling outside. The security guard came to report that the dismissed senior employee had come with his wife and sister-in-law, insisting they be admitted. They had come to see me and refused to leave until they did. I instructed the guard to confirm that the coordinator had spoken for me in court and would continue to speak for the project. I felt no need to talk to him. He could make an appointment for another day with the lawyer or coordinator.

I had nothing to say to him or the family. They were creating a public disturbance as school was in session, and his sister-in-law refused to stop yelling. She used exact phrases from my conversation with the vehement employee, who had a scheduled leave that day. The guard returned with the answer that they would not leave without speaking with me.

I told the guard to inform the group that they were trespassing since they had been asked to leave. If they refused, we would call the police. Most importantly, they stood on land connected to God's mission, and He was hearing their every word.

The guard said if he told her that, she would attack him. I asked him if he could call the police. It was unbelievable that he did not have their telephone numbers. I instructed the coordinator to correct this so that the police number was readily available to the guards in case of need in the future. I then asked him to telephone our lawyer for recommendations. The lawyer advised us to let him call the dismissed employee's lawyer and the police. We were to remain in place until he called back.

No one wanted a police intervention, so the guard and coordinator again spoke with the dismissed employee. Left alone, I walked across the hall, looked out the window, and saw the yelling woman. Feeling a move in my spirit, I prayed, "Please, God, make her leave. I rebuke her presence and the spirit inside her in the name of Jesus."

Immediately, the dismissed employee and his wife walked toward the small rear gate to exit our compound, and the yelling woman followed them. Once the three were outside, the gate was closed and bolted. Wow, I'd never prayed and seen a visible answer to my prayer like that. It was a miracle! The Holy Spirit had physically pushed them out the gate. *Thank God.*

I looked down at the surrounding houses. People were standing, listening in their doorways to what she was yelling. Some were laughing, entertained by what she said. They had missed what I had just experienced. I wanted to shout a question out of the window: Did you see what God did?

The dismissed employee was well-respected in the community. It was rumored he claimed he was in control of deciding who got into our programs and who got to work there. This was a lie, but many believed it. Unbelievably, some had a bad attitude toward the place that provided the highest-quality education for their children at the lowest cost in the area, as evidenced by our exam scores. Americans had sent money for the higher education of our school's graduates. They had willingly accepted this. Now, offering no words in our defense, they listened to this sister-in-law, yelling curses and threats against us as she walked away from our compound. I prayed again, "God, stop her mouth. Rebuke her lies. Stop her evil words." At that instant, she was silent and continued walking away. I saw the neighbors go inside their homes. The show was over. Wow, again. "Thank you, Lord, for answering my prayer," I mouthed.

At the sound of staff members' footsteps mounting the stairs, I walked back to the office. When they were all seated, I shared what I had prayed for and seen happen from my place by the window. I encouraged them to believe that God keeps his promises. I prayed that God would enable them to believe in His power and not be afraid of people. I thanked God for providing me with a clear and protected journey home and stood to leave.

Bolstered by this report and prayer, they happily escorted the coordinator and me to the car. The two teachers entered the car with us as the guard ran to open the large car entry gate. He waved, smiling as we departed. In my side mirror, I watched him cast furtive glances down the road as he closed the large gate quickly. I sighed, disappointed that he was still worried despite all that had happened. Maybe he was supposed to be apprehensive. He was the guard on duty.

We drove down the road past the walking family group. One young man was carrying a hoe. For some reason, the coordinator stopped the car to greet them. They returned the greeting. The sister-in-law stood waving, smiling, and saying the dismissed employee's name.

I asked the coordinator why he had stopped in the middle of the hostile group. He said it would have been disrespectful to refuse to greet people you recognized. To me, it seemed like a temptation to violence. We had been threatened. *Tradition runs deep.*

We continued to the main road without incident. Here, the two teachers descended as our paths headed in opposite directions. We headed toward town with few cars on the road. The coordinator said he'd never encountered such light traffic or made such rapid progress on this road. I reminded him that we had prayed for a protected passage home. God had more cleared the way.

Chapter 26

We made such good progress on the road that I decided to pass by to see my friend, who had decided she could not host me at her house. I called her, and we went to her home. I gave her my gift. I did not enter the house, but she was gracious enough to put me in touch with another former friend with book outlet contacts. She also had prepared a large garbage bag full of lovely stuffed animals. I was delighted, thinking about how precious these would be to the orphans who would typically not see something like this.

Sometimes, we think people are blocking us by not keeping their promises. But sometimes, an unkept promise, a broken trust, or betrayal banks our shot. If you have ever played billiards or pool, you know a ball can rebound in a different but desired direction when hit against the wall.

The place where I'd stayed initially was the best place to see visitors, have private discussions, and be close to the business district. My disappointment was redirected to an appreciation for God's provision and plan.

The following day, our lawyer called to report that he had arrived at the police station, only to find it locked. He thought the police on duty had left purposely to avoid being pulled into a community-dividing situation. Hoping cooler heads would win out, they had ignored the report the lawyer had alerted them he was coming to submit. He went back later, and eventually, the dismissed employee was arrested.

A few days later, the police called our lawyer and asked for mercy for the trespassing charge so they could release him. The dismissed employee was so sick they were afraid he would die in jail. He promised not to repeat the action and signed a decree witnessed by the lawyers and accepted by the court not to bring suit again. We agreed because our aim had been achieved by having him stay away from the school and out of court.

We were shocked to be notified that he had gone to another court jurisdiction and filed another suit against us. He was ungrateful for our mercy and lost the case. His decision made no sense to me, but that is what delusion is all about.

Because of his actions, we were made aware of the change in the law that now affected our organization. We agreed to start paying the required costs, and the DRC project status was updated to "in compliance." It ended up being for our benefit.

This was what God had promised. He is faithful even when it does not make sense to us at the time. You have two options when distracted by a few days of frustration, financial setbacks, relationship betrayal, or poor health. You can choose to fall into discouragement or depression, or you can also remain grounded in the belief that God has the power and willingness to keep His word and promise to make everything work to your benefit. Reality is not what you think and feel or how you respond to a situation. It is knowing to look beyond the appearance of circumstances to see what God says about them. That is the eternal truth.

When I first came to the DRC, I thought I had come for a two-week mission. On my return, I would stay for a limited time to develop the community's health capacity. The Tropical Disease Certificate was obtained to run the Nkamba Hospital, but it took me out of Nkamba due to the impending church split. The split in the church, which had extended the invitation allowing me to live and work in the DRC, caused my protective cover to crumble. I prepared to return to the US and restart by getting a job and sending money to support a project on unsure ground.

During this departure preparation, my insight developed into an urgent need that aligned with a calling from my earlier life: an orphanage. I had forgotten the dream, but God had not. He had brought the opportunity to build a project to address this issue in this place and time.

I planned to purchase a large house with land around it to construct a playground, kitchen garden, and other buildings as needed—my search for possible places brought to my attention one that seemed perfect. Fortunately, a lawyer from the church warned me of a scam being pulled on the unwary. When elderly parents of a family died, a designated child would be left in charge of finding a buyer for the house. The selling price was to be agreed on, and then the money was divided among the heirs.

However, what often happened was when a buyer was found, the family representative would sign the agreement without informing the other children or getting their signatures on the official agreement and leave, taking the money. The new purchaser could not occupy the house as the family was in the process of suing their representative for the title to gain authorization for the selling price and the distribution of the resulting money. My lawyer's research revealed this site fell into that category, saving us from a horrible situation.

I went from one end of town to the other, searching for a location for the orphanage. We could not find a building suiting our needs. While we continued to look for a place, a church pastor offered to help us find land to buy. He was such a dear man of God and exerted his influence in the community so that we could purchase titles for several plots for the project. At the time of purchase, the land was reasonably priced. The site was in a new area without utilities, roads, or many permanent housing developments. We would have to construct a building, which would delay starting, but we could design it to meet our needs. God had provided the job to support the construction and running of a project that changed the lives of widows, orphans, and schoolchildren in a new area. I had come to know from experience this saying was true: "There are no coincidences with God."

God arranged many miraculous events and experiences during the construction of the new school building. However, there were plenty of hurdles and disagreements. Some serious arguments led to my losing confidence in the team. I must stop working with them regarding the construction or lose my relationship with them as church brothers. I chose the former option.

When we started building the new school, we incurred high expenses and disagreements with the new team. I was not present because of my WHO job, but I knew God had provided the job for this purpose.

I intended to let the grant pay for the school's construction. When that fell through, I unsuccessfully tried different means to borrow the money. I would have to work to have enough money to run things as planned. But I was plagued by the question the church head had asked me: "Did God call you to be present or to bring the money to run the project?"

That is always a good question. At that time, I must admit God had told me to come. On arrival in Nkamba, all my needs were provided—housing, food, cooking, cleaning, and transportation. No salary had been provided, but there was no need for one. It was like manna. What I needed was always supplied. Once I'd left Nkamba, my means of support had been money from my home church in the States. Only when I'd started working regularly in Kinshasa did provision come through my employment.

How could I be sure He was not calling me to join the other donors now? Maybe it was time to leave the running in someone else's hands. Our roles and circumstances change as we grow older. This could be when God called me to leave the palace in Egypt behind for the sheep fields of Midian, like Moses. He could ask me to leave the sheep in Bethlehem and move to the palace in Jerusalem, like David. Perhaps I will not be able to complete the project like David, but I could arrange all the provisions and not be allowed to build His temple. How could I be sure of anything until I heard from God?

Chapter 27

California

How would it work now? I was not living in the DRC nor working as a full-time medical doctor. I would need more than my limited retirement income to pay for the running costs of the DRC project. In the back of my mind was the option of working a part-time job if needed. My medical license was still valid. There was also the possibility that an agent would recognize my next book as the gem they had been searching for. This picture proved faulty.

I was unaware that a box labeled "my control" was hidden in the corner of my heart. The box's existence, with its unstable and toxic content, became increasingly evident in the form of frustration and anxiety about financing the DRC project. Things were not going the way they should have. I searched for ways to supply the project's needs.

Subtly woven in the fabric of my life's tapestry was an assumption that I would be the solution to all of the DRC project's problems. God had given me a mandate and arranged a string of miracles to guide me to this point. As His servant, I was doing everything for His glory. I had pangs of conscience when people referred to it as my orphanage. I even caught myself calling it "my orphanage" when talking about what God was doing with the DRC project. Of course, I would quickly correct myself and others to remind all that it was God's project. Its success and achievements or failures were under His control.

One day, this hit me hard. I dropped to my knees and cried out to God to remove any of my delusions that things had ever been done or thought of without Him. Wasn't this the lesson I had come to understand on the mountaintop while looking back over the journey of the step, the jump over the crevasse, and then the climb? It had been God all along.

It was His wisdom and guidance that had brought me the opportunity to help these orphans. They had been brought to our door because there was a hope and future God wanted to reveal to and through them.

Nothing was working out. Why had I been able to submit everything to Him in the past but not now? The peace and joy I desired were not present this time. I asked God what was going on and to search my heart and let me see what was blocking His provision. Did I fully understand that the DRC project belonged to God entirely? He would do the best for the lives affected. He saw their hearts and the situation in minute detail. It was under His complete control. Out came the struggle to hold on to my control box. It needed to come out into the "Son light" and be exposed for what it was. I lacked trust in God to steer and fund the project without me. Who was this *me*?

The lid flew off the carefully hidden box. The image of my importance in providing for the DRC project shattered into tiny pieces around me as I remembered praying on the cement slab in the garden in Nkamba. That night, when I could have asked for anything in the world, my plea had been for God to provide the resources for what He had called me to do. Although He faithfully did that, I had started taking credit in small, ugly, and prideful ways. I was horrified that slipping off the road into a terrible ditch was so easy.

I agreed to accept what He was doing, His timing, and His power, not worry about what was happening, and listen to what I should do. I prayed that the prideful thinking that I could supply the project's needs would be removed. I acknowledged God's responsibility to provide for their needs on every level. This commitment required me to take another unexpected step because I did not understand how deep my pride ran. I still thought I had choices, but my imagined options were painfully stripped away.

A year after I resigned from my job, the renewal bill for my active medical license arrived. Living on a much-reduced income made the payment for the active license more than I could afford. By contrast, the cost of the retired license category was quite affordable. This would mean no longer giving medical advice or working as a healthcare provider, even part-time. I had not worked for a year and didn't know if I ever would as I continued writing. At present, there was no option. By putting a small check in a box, I became a retired medical doctor and became, by default, a full-time writer. I left the licensing board office feeling like I'd just lost a large part of myself. But it was strange there was no grief for the loss.

For years, giving medical advice in response to symptoms and health questions had become second nature to me. When presented with symptoms, my response had been to start making a list of possible diagnoses immediately and ask further questions to whittle the list down to a few possibilities. Then, the decision would be to order more detailed tests to confirm a diagnosis or refer to a specialist. My actions and words were confident, authoritative, and respected. Then, one day after registering as a retired physician, I could no longer provide official medical advice.

I had not suddenly lost the ability to apply everything I had seen and learned for many years. However, I understood the intent of this rule since the retired status has no requirements for updating medical education. Without attending updating practice regulation sessions or discussions with colleagues, one could quickly become outdated.

The choice was clear. I could no longer oscillate between my career choices. I had to submit to the call to make a living and focus on writing. The focus part was only a personal decision. Earning an income would require engaging with many people and either getting a publisher or the money to self-publish and market my books. That would take some doing.

God sent the help I needed in an extraordinary way. Calls from former colleagues started coming almost daily with questions. Beneath their medical questions were unspoken requests for reassurance. The reasons for their need for reassurance were varied.

Had they chosen the right field? If someone with my level of medical skills was leaving the field, was there something they needed to know about the future? What should be done to restore their joy of occupation?

These were spiritual questions, and I focused on asking them about their center of balance, the basis of moral strength, and their choice of internal life goals that could withstand changes in their surrounding circumstances. My advantage was age and experience. I had asked myself many of the same questions over the years and understood that at the base of their questions was a more narrow and valid question about truth. These discussions brought back memories of past experiences and lessons learned. I shared these memories with them to show that everyone faces grave life issues. But no matter how challenging the way seems, we gain the courage to press on and overcome when someone we know succeeds. Hearing about one of my previous experiences often proved to be a strong enough breeze to blow away the clouds of discouragement that were blocking the sunny joy from their day. This allowed my stories and memories to stay at the top of my mind and help me. Unfortunately, it would often only take a small amount of doubt to create an immersing environment of discouragement.

Science shows us a dense fog covering seven city blocks to a depth of one hundred feet, composed of less than one glass of water. That amount of water is divided into about sixty billion tiny droplets. When these settle over a city or the countryside, they blot everything from sight. Just one glass of water can cause several accidents, such as its impact. We can rise a few flights into the joyous sunshine above ground level or wait until the fog clears. The cold, wet, and dim fog of discouragement clears with time. Three books started pouring out of me about issues raised in conversations with colleagues and friends and are some of my best works to date.

***

I was allowing new guidance from God with a focus on the DRC orphans. I asked God what He wanted me to do. He brought each child's face before my closed eyes and reminded me that these were His children. I was to teach them about God's love at every possible opportunity, so they would choose to give their lives to serve Him and those around them. He had given me the same plan for my actions with my children. It was the foundation of any other choices, the armor that would protect them anywhere they went.

We had bought French Bibles and Bible storybooks for bedtime stories and morning prayer. The entire school staff began each morning and ended each school day with prayer. We asked our international prayer partners to pray for us to hear God's direction.

Some of the children were becoming teenagers and needed specific and additional instruction. A download in my spirit showed me various ways to use our present financial situation to reveal some organizational restructuring of the project. Our financial restrictions revealed the intents and priorities of some staff members, allowing downsizing as people resigned.

Chapter 28

If I had met my three children as adults for the first time, they would have quickly become cherished acquaintances. But having raised them, I know the precious-gem quality of their characters. They possess generous hearts, joyful spirits, hope in the face of adversity, and quick wits. This was, in part, because their childhood had been a touch-and-go journey for us as a family.

They had gone for court-ordered visits with their father and half-siblings on some weekends and school holidays. When I was at medical school, we had lived in the same city, and it was emotionally trying to hear tearful stories of their visits. Due to the four-hour drive distance, moving to my specialty residency program also made it physically demanding to drop them off at their father's place. Their father would pick them up, and I would retrieve them. It was a taxing trip for me, often after a night on call with little sleep. Sometimes, I stopped for a nap at my mom's house, letting the kids play with their cousins. I prayed, knowing this was a three-year medical residency and thus entailed that length of struggle for all of us.

In an angry mood, one day, their father called me. He declared it was my fault the children were reticent to visit him. He threatened to sue me for custody as I would be a wealthy doctor soon, and he would gladly take my money to pay for their support. It was evident he had given this some thought as he claimed these were reasonable grounds.

He also claimed I was so career-hungry and busy that I did not have time to spend with my children. At the same time, he had a two-parent home where neither parent worked. I didn't want to believe the court would give him custody, but the world was ridiculous. This bothered me deeply, not only because of my love for my kids but also because of how they suffered when staying with him.

I found myself crying every time I woke up, increasingly anxious that he might be preparing to initiate legal action. Then, to my relief, a message came to me—through a dream. In this dream, I saw a slimy, muddy-bottomed pond in a cool, shaded area with lily pads on its surface. Seeing its moldy edges was disgusting. As I neared it, I saw a shallow corner where something was squirming around in the muddy bottom. Shivering with aversion, I turned to walk away and caught sight of something out of the corner of my eye. A bright white-water lily sat near the center on a green pad. It was fresh and pristine, with no mark or trace of the filthy mud or slimy mold surrounding it.

An involuntary whisper of awe escaped my lips, "How beautiful."

A tender voice said, "Yes, I have this flower blossoming in my honor for only a few days, to stand without a trace of the filth around it. Why do you think I could not do that with these precious children? They are mine wherever they are and will reflect my glory. Your job is to teach them about me, their Heavenly Father."

With a long exhale, all anxiety left me, and that day, my life perspective changed. If I were supposed to be the teacher of God's children, I would use every opportunity to point out His presence and handiwork around us. No time would be wasted in letting my children know their responsibility toward their Heavenly Father. They were, after all, His children, and I was their teacher for an unknown period. Fortunately, their father never sued me for custody. However, the transformation in my mind of my role in their lives profoundly impacted us. That image of what God can do in the most horrible situations was indelibly recorded in my mind.

I also began to reflect on the many heroes mentioned in the Bible who have left us testimonies of God's method of carrying out His will in their lives. Abraham, the friend of God, was renamed to reflect the promise to be the father of a great nation. He only saw one of these promised babies born before he died. Moses was called to lead his people to freedom. He was allowed to see the promised land from a distance but did not walk into the land before he died. Daniel, a prophet, was shown, through visions, the birth and second return of Jesus Christ. Daniel saw neither fulfilled before his death. It may have seemed to them and us today that their missions were incomplete before he died. But these men did what they were called to do.

My dad dreamed of a small clinic to serve the people of our area, a canyon with a small population. He never saw the dream fulfilled. After his death, several others took the dream and gradually expanded the idea to five clinics serving a population of over two hundred thousand with primary, nonemergency healthcare in the third largest city in Los Angeles County. People also come to these clinics from the surrounding distant towns.

We gauge the feasibility of projects within the timeframe of our one human lifetime. We like neat, definable, and complete missions with a beginning and end that fall between our birth and death dates. Only God has the complete forever view. This is His story and not our story.

I remembered two distinct events while I lived in Kenya in the early eighties. I had been asked to come to this poor school built by local parents to educate their children. A community leader and teacher had gotten permission to seek a college-certified teacher to teach there and be paid by the Ministry of Education. I had agreed to prepare and was enrolled for the following term to live and teach there in a rural area. My house had no indoor plumbing. My salary was around two hundred dollars a month. I had to walk everywhere, even at times uphill into town, which was almost two miles away, but the community was warm and gracious.

After two years, the government notified me that my contract was canceled and my visa revoked, requiring a mandatory departure. This shocked everyone as I was the school's only qualified teacher. We asked around, trying to understand why.

It was rumored that young Kenyans and recent graduates at the teacher's college had protested to the Ministry of Education. They claimed they could not find jobs as teachers because international noncitizens occupied them. To avoid a scandal, a commitment was made to rectify the situation. The Minister of Education decided to take the evidence presented and fire all expatriate teachers in the country. I left for California with my two babies. My husband, who was working at a private university, was not affected by this declaration and hoped to find a way to have us return under a different visa to rejoin him.

Many of the expatriates had taught at rural schools. They had a philanthropic spirit and had come to live in rural locations as teachers for years. After receiving the notice, many looked for jobs in neighboring countries. Others retired and returned to homes far away. Their rush to comply with the order resulted in a mass exodus. Neighboring countries were glad to receive them.

Unfortunately for Kenya, within a month, it was apparent that many young Kenyan protesters were unwilling to be assigned to the posts vacated in the rural schools. They wanted to live in towns. A crisis was created in schools across the nation. The rural schools did not recover for some time. New expatriate teachers were brought in, and others were invited to return. I happily returned to the same school.

My students made history with their national test scores, unexpected from a community-supported school. This triggered my transfer to a government school at the start of the new term. For those left behind, it was the same as if I'd left the country, although it was to live in a city a few hours away. I was convinced I had done my best in the given time, but my heart felt I had not completed my task. The following year, I left the country for personal reasons. When I returned many years later, I had no desire to visit my old school. But I was told I should see it because of the good news.

The school had drawn much attention because my students' national exam scores had been so good in science the year I left. There was also a national rule that no school on the national map would be allowed to downsize its staff and supplies. Two government-salaried teachers had been sent to replace me in the first year. Classroom labs had been built, and dormitories had been added. Three more government-salaried teachers were assigned after that. The school had become famous and attracted students from far and wide. They had thrived after my kick start and then departure. They had been given an incredible opportunity after we had won a victory. It showed me that whether we hear about the results or not, obedience is honored by God. This was a lesson that reappeared many times in my life.

***

It seemed familiar when I heard about the DRC's nationwide declaration of free primary education. My thoughts flew back to that experience in Kenya. Of course, it's too early to see the result. But I thought about how I would have implemented the changeover to free primary education. I know nothing of the deadlines, parameters, funding, agreements, or other limits affecting the decision. I can only consider what I learned and how it affected those I knew, a common mistake of human beings. We are very nearsighted, and unlike chickens, we cannot see what is happening on the sides of our path.

Hope and perseverance can yield huge harvests. The same thing done at different times can produce different results. I pray that God guides the national leaders to find a Godly solution so that students will not suffer a delay in education or a decreased literacy rate in the country. Long experience has reminded me that there is a reason for everything. I also pray that God guides us as we manage the DRC project from the humanly visible side. We have already had some revelations about the adjustments we need to make in the orphanage.

Once the proposals were presented, I was told that others had suggested some of the same changes on visitation reports. I was surprised to hear about these suggestions for the first time, but I was glad God had brought them to light. He will find a means to shine His light on a topic, start an activity, or stop an action. We are expected to work without imposing our agendas or resisting His. After all, He is responsible for the results, and His way is always far better.

God has the power and creativity to grow a water lily in a slimy pond. He can also change our point of view to benefit those around us. The water lily story has helped many see the truth, as it did me. By taking our eyes off the surrounding slime and mold, we can focus on what God has promised to do.

***

The DRC government school inspectors told us that we needed to keep up with the required increase in capacity to accept new students. The problem was that we needed adequate classroom space to expand our intake. We used the last of our donations to repurpose the auditorium into six classrooms in time for the new term. Parents enrolled, and it appeared that we would be able to break even. We let the parents pay in installments. We opened our first year of the seventh through ninth-grade level and envisioned a shift toward self-sufficiency for the school that year.

242

Chapter 29

In early 2024, it was a shock to be informed that the DRC government had declared primary school education free for all children in grades one through six, with immediate effect. The country went from fee-based to free education in the middle of the school year. Most schools like ours had agreed with parents for an installment-based payment plan because it was difficult for them to pay the year's tuition all at once. There was a sudden loss of income as parents did not honor their promises for payment. Yet they continued to send their children to class to be taught by the same teachers they were no longer paying. There was no way for nongovernment-sponsored schools to pay out money for salaries and supplies with this sudden loss of revenue. Schools were forbidden to close or require parents to pay these fees. We had heard of no plan to negotiate this problem.

If we had known about the educational plan, we might have spent less on repurposing construction but held it back for salaries. If fees were fully paid, we might have decided to start the term with only two hundred students. Life is replete with instances where, had we known something, we would have made other choices. It is so good to remember that God knows everything and has it all under control.

We also knew that our oldest orphans would take their national sixth-grade exams at the end of the 2024 school year. The cost of tuition, boarding, transportation to a distant campus, and its psychological and social impact would be challenging in many ways.

Because of the new declaration, we were facing a preschool through sixth-grade school closure for this next year. We could still charge parents of the seventh and eighth graders to pay for their teachers' salaries. We would have to find an arrangement for the classes for our younger twelve orphans and employees' children. This could mean we would shoulder the cost of sending our orphans to schools outside our compound for the first time and the prelude to another miracle.

The project seemed to be shrinking to survive. This was not what I'd expected. There were so many questions. *Had I not understood the dream? Was it wrong to expect parents to keep their promises made at the beginning of the school year? We had done so much to make their lives better. Was it incorrect to be disappointed by politicians who expected supporters of an improved society to be obstructed from their ability to continue to do so?*

I remembered the journalist's words in Nkamba on my first day. "We will see if God brings this baby back to life."

It's interesting that in the darkest, most silent part of the night, we often hear God's voice speaking to our hearts the clearest.

***

Some of us see our life's race as an individual competition in its various stages, where we strive to be among the first three to finish, the physically strongest, or the top of our class in school or the job. We hope to receive a personal award for performing better than others in some way. We are focused on pleasing God with a well-run and finished race based on the criteria of most incredible faith, a servant's heart, and creativity in music or art. But could we be straying off target by comparing our efforts to others?

God calls *us* to be the best versions of ourselves that he has created us to be. He took the time to prepare us for His purpose in our location, age, and even our character. No, we aren't perfect, but we are perfect for the job we are called to do. Even our continued refinement is a testimony to His plan.

I have begun to view my effort as part of a relay team. In the race of my life, I received a warm baton from the hands of another. For a while, my lane took me through the DRC. I waited, anticipating the baton, then firmly seized and ran with it.

In relay sports, this is called "a blind pass": The first runner enters the changeover zone at full speed and judges when the second runner is up to speed. The second runner stretches his open hand backward. Once the baton is placed in his hand, the second runner firmly grasps it and whips away to continue the race. Having run with all his might to this point, the first runner knows that failure or success is now "out of his hands." It is up to the second runner to be diligent for the next leg. The first runner makes his way off the track to join the audience in cheering his team on to victory.

One part of the race needs the gift of being strong, organized, creative, and steady to maintain progress. The next runner may have opposite gifts necessary for that part of the race and run differently. They may be gifted to run as fast as the wind, a trait needed for the success of the last leg. That may be why the time will come to pass the responsibility on.

Just allow that to sink in. It is the slowest runner that hands the baton to the fastest runner. What a contrast, but the anchor has an idea of the effort he must exert to regain the time lost during the other three legs of the race.

Though not the first runner in this kingdom relay race, my part of the race is all I know— the only part I need to know. I was born to run this leg, this section. My God-given abilities, talents, and training uniquely qualify me for this part of the relay race. My second-guessing and what-ifs are set aside. I'm not too old or young. I have the life experience for this task at this exact time and place, making me the perfect candidate.

Any hesitation in my steps now would not be because I doubt who God is or what He can do. I must be sure I clearly hear and diligently carry out His will. As a scientist, I depend on logic, intellect, and strategy. But God continues to reveal that his loving hand is all-powerful. His wisdom surpasses anything we could ever understand in this earthly life, and He sees into the very hearts of all men. He controls the universe and worlds beyond our discovery.

Whenever it seems the world is swirling in confusion, chaos, and evil imaginings, I reset my focus on God's will and find a clear path through the fray. Any fear is calmed by a reminder that I am not alone but in the company of the almighty God. He is the God of miracles. Nothing, and yet everything, makes sense: healings, prison doors flying open, joy while being chained to guards in a dungeon, the crucifixion, and resurrections.

This is His world, every particle of it. The DRC project is a tiny dot in the mosaic of God's blueprint. He takes full responsibility because He has complete control. Our close-up view does not give us the complete picture and is thus often hard to accept. It's not my task to shoulder the responsibility of whether or not I lived to see all the DRC project's orphans or even my grandchildren become adults. This thought causes me to take a deep sigh. At the same time, I pray, believing that I may see another miracle any minute or that God has a different, much better plan.

Could I change anything if I knew His plan and disagreed with it? No. So, why not acknowledge that God has always had the perfect plan and has covered all the bases? He completes everything He starts. The closer we walk with Him, letting Him direct our steps, the more precise the path of victory appears in our lives.

Although saved by God's mercy and grace, being human, I tend to forget that I am not called to do a task to the best of my ability but called to allow Him to work through me. Whatever else I do on a given day, walking and talking with Him is the most important thing.

There will be no need for second-guessing when we're in constant conversation. The fact that I cherish our relationship and His presence allows my joy to overflow no matter where we go. So, my peace is not disturbed even in the darkest places and most difficult circumstances. Everything is on purpose and for His purpose. There are no coincidences with God.

The orphanage in the DRC project is an ongoing miracle, and I am running my leg in that relay race. I have been blessed to experience many miracles, which have prepared me for this present part of the great race. There have been miracles during the race that urged me to continue to run. It is my pleasure and mandate to share the stories about the miracles I recognize. There are others I did not realize were happening at the time. I will write about them if they come to mind. It's all proof that it was never me but His might all along.

I still haven't understood whether my first jump landed in Nkamba since it happened so long ago and seems so far away. But I am determined to enjoy all the aspects of wherever I find myself with the view, the people, and the task at hand. Perhaps there have been several mountaintop landings since the first command to "jump" on the way to Nkamba. Commands may have come, and my response had been automatic.

Twenty-two years seems like a long time to be soaring between mountain tops, but I don't know much about how those things work. I can't imagine the views and accomplishments since then were visible in the distance from Nkamba to anyone except God. There's a lot beyond my ability to imagine or ask for, and God has provided far more than that. Papa signaled the launch of my unlimited mission. Yes, I'm concerned about what is happening, but I'm convinced God's answer comes at the right time and in the right way. This is who He is and what He does. I crouch at a moment's notice, ready to "jump" when I hear the command.

I hope reading through this slice of my life inspires you to avoid letting **yourself** be the limiting factor in fulfilling **your** life's calling. We make better progress when we stop trying to grab control of the steering wheel from the passenger seat as if we know our destination.

He may speak to me in bright flashes of ideas, dreams, and visions because He has made my receiver sensitive to other things requiring that. You may hear a small voice. However we hear, we must listen and obey.

God shows His power through us. Let God's power and willingness to perform miracles through you be revealed to those around you. It is for His glory. The unbelievable becomes authentic when you see what God is doing in your life and tell others about it.